THE END OF THE WORLD
IS A CUL DE SAC

THE END OF THE WORLD IS A CUL DE SAC

Louise Kennedy

BLOOMSBURY PUBLISHING

LONDON · OXFORD · NEW YORK · NEW DELHI · SYDNEY

BLOOMSBURY PUBLISHING
Bloomsbury Publishing Plc
50 Bedford Square, London, WC1B 3DP, UK
29 Earlsfort Terrace, Dublin 2, Ireland

BLOOMSBURY, BLOOMSBURY PUBLISHING and the Diana logo are
trademarks of Bloomsbury Publishing Plc

First published in Great Britain 2021

A catalogue record for this book is available from the British Library

ISBN: HB: 978-1-5266-2327-0; TPB: 978-1-5266-2328-7;
EBOOK: 978-1-5266-2329-4

2 4 6 8 10 9 7 5 3
4 6 8 10 9 7 5

Typeset by Integra Software Services Pvt. Ltd
Printed and bound in Great Britain by CPI Group (UK) Ltd, Croydon CR0 4YY

To find out more about our authors and books visit www.bloomsbury.com
and sign up for our newsletters

For my mother and father

CONTENTS

THE END OF THE WORLD IS
A CUL DE SAC

The dereliction was almost beautiful, the houses dark
against the mauve dawn, pools of buff-coloured water
glinting briefly as a passing car took the last bend before
town. Number 7 was starting to look like the other units,
the lawn stringy with brown weeds. The footpath petered
out and Sarah landed hard in a puddle, picking her way
over broken masonry and loops of cable until she reached
the end of the cul de sac. The noise was coming from the
show house. It looked even worse inside than out. Clots
of dung littered the travertine floor. All the doors had
been taken, including the front one, which only seemed
to emphasise how small the rooms were. The donkey was
in the living room, by the cavity in the chimney breast
where the granite fireplace had been. It was plump and
skittish, pastilles of dried sleep at the corners of its eyes.
Sarah whispered to it, cajoled, pleaded. She tried shoo-
ing it, spreading her arms to drive it out to the hallway.
It pawed and snattered, and a flume of shit hit the wall
behind it. She would have to go and get her neighbour.

She left the estate and started up the steep lane towards Mattie Feeney's house. She had gone there once with Davy, when the old man's wife died. Away from the main road the light was different. It was hard to see. The brambles that coiled back over the dry-stone walls nicked her hands. She walked faster, almost trotting, her wellingtons kicking up small rocks and squeaking over the tranche of grass that ran the centre of the lane. She was breathing hard when she reached the yard. A light was on in the stables. Someone was mucking out, metal tines scraping the ground. The raking stopped. She didn't hear footsteps until they were very close.

You're up early, said a voice behind her. A man's voice, his accent local, from the town.

I can't see you, she said, turning quickly.

The speaker was barely thirty, with a clipped beard and hair brushed to one side. The thin electric light made him look drawn.

Did I scare you? he said to her hands. She looked at them. They were trembling.

One of the donkeys got out. She wasn't used to hearing herself speak and her voice sounded slight, inconsequential.

Where is it?

In the show house.

I see, he said. His eyes were laughing at her.

Should I go and tell Mattie?

He's up in the hospital.

Is he all right?

He had a stroke three weeks ago.

I didn't know. How is he?

The speech wasn't affected. He'll be back when they finish the physio.

He hooked a horsebox on to an old jeep and opened the passenger door. You might show me where the donkey is, he said. She sat beside him. There was a tree-shaped air freshener swinging from the rear-view mirror, but the jeep had the sweet, gamey odour of animals. At the bottom of the lane he glanced up and down the road, his eyes lingering on her when he looked left.

Ryan is my name, he said.

Sarah.

I know, he said. You're the gangster's moll from down the hill.

Is that what they call me?

I'm after thinking of it now.

She got out by the entrance and unchained the gate, swinging it open to let the jeep in. Ryan pulled in beside a dome of polished granite that had been sandblasted with the words HAWTHORN CLOSE in a Celtic font that Sarah had thought at the time might tempt fate. Not that she had told Davy so.

Morning had broken. Under the low cloud, the sunflower-yellow paint on the houses appeared noxious.

I thought the place looked bad from the road, he said. She followed him to the show house. He sidestepped the shit and stood in the kitchen. There wasn't much left of it. Mould-speckled French-Grey paint, dangling wires. Buckled skirting boards and sawn-off pipes. A few days before Davy left, a contractor had called to their house and accused him of stripping the place himself, selling the fittings on the sly. Sarah had run the man from the door; now she was inclined to believe him.

Ryan went into the living room. He ruffled the donkey's mane. All right, buddy, he said.

I didn't know what to do, said Sarah. I think I just frightened him.

He gave its arse a slap. The animal shimmied and clopped then began to move, colliding with walls and doorframes, reeling back before Ryan got it out the front. He jollied and pushed it across the hardcore, leaning his weight on it to get it into the horsebox. He secured the door and put his hands on his hips. Fuck's sake, he said, the words leaving his mouth like steam.

I can close the gate after you and walk up.

I said I'd drop you home, he said, getting into the jeep. Sarah understood. He was offering her a lift because he wanted to see the house. Everyone wanted to see the house. Strangers rang the bell on vague pretexts. Selling calendars. Asking for directions. Straining their necks to look into the hall when Sarah opened the door. Walking around the side for a view of the housing estate her husband had thrown up and abandoned to her.

Ryan waited while she locked the gate. She sat back in the passenger seat and he watched her pull the safety belt across herself. They only had two hundred yards to travel, but it made her feel bolstered, held in place. Her driveway bent up in an arc that mirrored the line of the floating wall at the front. The horsebox swung left and right, and Ryan had to lock hard to park.

She opened the front door. Bills and fliers were strewn across the entrance hall. The art was gone, lifted off the walls by the owner of the gallery on a tip-off from the architect. Davy had taken the buffalo hide he had bought when he went to the Super Bowl. It was the only thing he took with him.

Some spot, said Ryan.

His voice was still wobbling in the high, empty space as they entered the kitchen.

Coffee? she asked.

Aye, go on.

She filled the kettle and got out mugs and a jar of instant granules. He moved around the room, taking it in. The dining table was glass and chrome and surrounded by twelve curved white chairs. A globular light fitting was suspended above it, a spiky metal Telstar sort of thing. The kitchen units were at floor level only, high-gloss white with walnut counters. Sarah had had

no hand in the decor. Davy had said it was the architect's job.

A vast patio door, bleared with dust, ran the length of
the dining table. Ryan tried the handle. Pull it right up
until it clicks, said Sarah. He opened the lock and slid
it across until it vanished into the wall. The room filled
with autumn. The must of leaf mould, the complaints of
robins. You could see over Mattie's place and across the
glen to the mountain. It was like being outside.

He leaned in the doorframe and lit a cigarette. His
shoulders were taut, as though he was trying to look
smaller. The beard both became him and made him
unremarkable. Sarah handed him his coffee. He lifted
the mug to his mouth and swallowed. He pulled a face
and inclined his head at the Bakelite coffee machine
that was plumbed in near the sink. How come I got the
cheap shite?

You can only get the pods online.

So get them online.

My cards were cancelled.

He stepped on to the patio and Sarah followed him
around to the west side of the house. She stood behind
him as he looked down the garden. Terraces of shrubs
were growing thickly all the way down to the wire fence,
the spherical shape the gardener had once imposed on the
box trees blurred with new shoots, the lavender silvery
and woody and still flowering. Hawthorn Close was

beyond it, lollipop-shaped: twelve semi-detached houses either side of a track that led to five detached houses around the bulb of a cul de sac. From here you could see things you couldn't see from the road. That one of the units had been occupied, that someone had tried to tame a garden and make a home. That the granite dome which read HAWTHORN CLOSE had been deposited on to a fairy fort. That beside the dome a tree had been torn down, its roots leaving deep velvety furrows which seemed to bulge when light fell across them.

Imagine living there, he said, turning to look at her. Sarah went back into the kitchen.

He followed her in and opened the fridge. It was empty except for Rouge Noir nail polish, skimmed milk and a prune yoghurt. He closed it again. Do you want to get out of here later? Get a drink or something? he said.

I don't know.

I'll come back at seven. He poured his coffee into the sink and left through the hall. She stood at the front door to see him off. He opened his window and adjusted his wing mirror. He was looking at her as he drove away.

After he left, she tied her hair up. She swept the floor. She wiped down all the surfaces in the kitchen and washed and dried the dishes. She closed the patio door and sprayed a section of the glass with green liquid she found in the utility room. She wiped it with newspaper and stood back. It looked worse than before. She sprayed the dining table and began buffing, rubbing round and round until the paper disintegrated. She cleaned the sink with bleach and mopped the tiles.

She went to the garden with the prune yoghurt and a teaspoon. She sat on a metal deckchair and ate, sucking the spoon clean after each mouthful. A car pulled in by the gate of the estate. The driver got out. He had greased-back red hair and an off-the-rack suit. He stuck his phone through the railings to take photographs. Before he drove off he made a call, his voice indistinct. He was probably from the bank, or from a firm of solicitors acting for a contractor who was owed money. The reporters had stopped coming, although she feared they would return after the inquest.

She ran her wedding finger around the inside of the pot and licked it. Her rings were loose. Her skin tasted of sour milk and chlorine and green apples. At least the place was clean. Maybe she should clean herself up too, in case Ryan came back. She went inside. She had started sleeping in the boot room Davy had built off the kitchen for their sons to use after football training. The arrogance seemed spectacular now; they didn't have sons, or daughters. The morning they found the body, Sarah had abandoned the master bedroom and dragged a mattress downstairs. Now she lay every night under the high shallow window with the white blind. There were grey stone slabs on the floor. The modular shelving that ran along one wall was empty. It resembled a clinic you saw on television where rich women went to lose weight or go mad.

She shampooed her hair and smeared the contents of a sample sachet of conditioner on to the ends, twisting it in a coil on the crown of her head. She shaved her legs and underarms. She hesitated then soaped between her legs, dragging the razor from back to front until her pubic hair lay in fuzzy clumps in the plughole. She wrapped herself in a towel and sat on the toilet seat with a magnifying mirror and tweezers, pulling black hairs from her moustache and eyebrows. The tubes and bottles of make-up in the bathroom cabinet were marked to be used within six months. They had gone off, like the prune yoghurt. She took out make-up brushes she had bought in Saks on Fifth Avenue – after a boozy lunch, for $314 – and applied liquids and gels and powders. When she was done, her skin was bronzed and dewy, her eyes dark and wide. She blow-dried her hair and wound it around electric rollers. When she was dressed she made a cup of tea and brought it outside. She sat in the metal deckchair again, a Missoni scarf on her head to hold the rollers in place, and waited.

At seven Ryan rapped a knuckle against the patch in the patio door she had tried to clean. Sarah saw her reflection. Her make-up had softened but there was no mistaking the care she had taken. She let him in. He smelled of deodorant and was wearing a fine wool jacket and expensive brogues. Maybe he had taken care too. He pointed at the smudged glass.

Was it all too much for you?

Ha, she said.

Are you hungry?

Not really. Her stomach made a hollow fizzle, betraying her.

Come on. I'll buy you a bit of dinner.

He had arrived in a silver convertible with leather seats. Very flash, she said. There was a fur of moss where the soft top met the window.

You're calling me flash? he said. Sarah turned to him, smiling. He wasn't smiling back.

She was stricken by her own foolishness. She didn't even know him. Besides, who was she kidding? She couldn't sit opposite a man at a table in this town. She hadn't so much as stood on High Street since Davy left. When the town was asleep, she bought milk and cut-price ham in the 24-hour petrol station with the dwindling bundle of notes she had found in Davy's wardrobe. I don't know if this is a good idea, she said.

Relax, he said. He had bypassed the town centre and was following signs for Dublin.

Where are we going?

I'm taking you for a spin. I'll have you home before midnight.

The short stretch of dual carriageway narrowed into a road without verges. They passed wooden crosses, sometimes alone, sometimes in twos and threes, that marked the sites of fatal crashes. He drove fast, even on hairpin bends where most drivers would have braked, his left hand splayed on the gearstick, fingers flexing and tensing, the rush doing something almost kinetic to him. He turned left at a derelict filling station and drove a couple of miles down a gentle hill. He parked behind a line of cars at a lakeside pub. An extractor fan was belching frying smells into the night. Sarah crossed the road to a jetty that protruded over the lake like a diving board. A band of the water was white with moonlight, small boats rocking and bumping together.

Inside they were seated near a gas fire that had fake coals intended to look like embers. A young waitress came with menus and listed the specials. Ryan ordered a shandy, and a glass of Prosecco for Sarah. She would have preferred a gin and tonic but didn't say so.

How long have you been working for Mattie?

He's my grandfather.

I didn't know that, she said. There was a story about one of Mattie's grandchildren, something Davy had told her. She couldn't remember what it was. The waitress put the drinks in front of them, Ryan's first.

He ordered dinner for them both, the most expensive dishes on the menu. Buttered Dublin Bay prawns with garlic chives. Organic fillet steak, well done. Sarah asked the waitress if she could have hers medium rare.

Why not? said Ryan. Maybe he wasn't used to eating in restaurants. Mattie was a bit of a hillbilly, and his grandson probably wasn't much better, with his townie accent and pointy shoes. Still, who would bring you out for dinner and then choose your food, your drink? It wasn't that Sarah disliked what he had ordered. Two steaks were carried to the next table and they looked and smelled delicious. But it was odd not to be asked what she wanted.

The waitress brought their starter. They ate in silence, Sarah using her fingers and finishing so fast she was ashamed. Hunger was hard to conceal when there was food in front of you. The main course arrived: two unstable stacks of charred meat, portobello mushroom, grilled beef tomato, and onion rings, served on wooden boards that had to be held with two hands. The manager carried Ryan's.

She'll have a glass of red with the beef, he said. Sarah tried to put aside the feeling he had taken charge of her. The food was good, the wine not bad either. It was nice to sit at a table in a restaurant. She'd had worse nights. When their plates were cleared, Sarah leaned back and smiled. Her belly was quiet for the first time in weeks.

Back in a sec, she said, and picked up her handbag. Ryan reached across and took her free hand. She knew what he had put in her palm before he closed her fingers around it. She crossed the room to the ladies and shut herself into the largest cubicle. She crunched out a line with one of the cancelled cards. He had given her a fifty-euro note too. She rolled it up and leaned over the cistern.

When she came out she looked in the mirror. The light in the bathroom was filtering through a red shade and should have been flattering. Her face was skull-like. There were purplish ruts under her eyes and a pair of deep grooves ran from either side of her nose to the corners of her mouth. She applied more concealer and eyeliner and fluffed out her hair. She put her hand on the door to leave. Then she turned quickly and went back into the cubicle. Another bump and she might even enjoy herself.

She sat demurely and smiled at Ryan, nudging his knee gently under the table to pass him the wrap and the banknote.

He spread his hands. That's for you, he said. He beckoned the waitress and ordered her another glass of red.

Why thank you, Sarah said when the drink arrived.

What's the story with your house? he said.

The bank is trying to sell it.

How's that going?

How do you think?

Why did you build the estate so close to your own place?

Davy was in trouble. He thought he could turn the development around fast, generate some cash flow.

Ryan gave a short laugh. He was in trouble, all right. What did you think?

I thought it would look ugly. That it was a huge risk. But he didn't ask me.

But you didn't say anything?

I'm the kind of girl men order dinner for, she said. Connaught's answer to Lauren Bacall or what? Fuck it. She was in the mood for some craic. She took a drink of her wine and waited for him to reply.

You seemed to be enjoying it, he said, a flash of something in the way he answered that made her stay quiet. She took another drink and looked around the room. Farmers and solicitors. Overdressed young couples. The usual frumpy lot you'd see in any restaurant down the country on a Friday night. Nosy as well, half of them gawping over and whispering. When Ryan spoke again he had composed himself. What about the estate? he said.

The receiver will accept a hundred grand for it.

Where's your husband?

There have been sightings of him in Malaga. Apparently.

The waitress came with dessert menus. I'm full, said Sarah. Ryan ordered her a crème brûlée. When it arrived she tapped at the caramel with the back of a teaspoon.

It cracked into shards that were shiny like tortoise shell. She pushed the dish away.

Ryan went to the bar to pay. The manager seemed to be apologising to him, gesticulating with her hands as she spoke. She called the young waitress over. The girl was short and Ryan had to bend to speak to her. He whispered in her ear then put something in her hand, closing her fingers around it the way he had earlier with the coke. She leapt up and kissed his cheek, fleeing to the kitchen. Ryan came back to the table with a carrier bag of clinking bottles.

What was that about?

Ould cunt didn't want me to give the girl a tip. Said the staff did all right with the service charge.

Sarah stood to put her jacket on. Every single person in the room was looking at her. They recognised her. It was why she didn't leave the house any more. People remembered her face from the papers. From the photograph of her and Davy the day she won the best-dressed prize at the Galway Races. Or worse, the one taken the day Eoin and Lizzie moved into Hawthorn Close. Herself and Lizzie in the centre, laughing, the baby leaning out of Lizzie's arms. Davy and Eoin flanking them, the yellow paint cheery in the sunshine. But was that why they were staring? There was something about Ryan, nothing overt, but it was there all the same, in the deference the manager showed him, the blushes of the waitress, as if she was star-struck. Was it the sight of them together that was such a spectacle? She didn't know. All she knew was that she was sick of being stared at by bogtrotters. She pulled her collar up and began striding towards the door. She was at the jetty when Ryan came out. He put the bag of bottles in the car and twisted her around to face him.

What's eating you? he said.

They were all looking at us.

Why would they be doing that?

I don't bloody know.

I'd say you've a fair idea.

What's that supposed to mean?

He laughed. You're gas, he said.

She sat in the car and opened the glove compartment. She did a line off the manual. There were CDs in a pouch. She found a compilation of seventies funk and put it on. On the road back to town she moved her shoulders to the music. When they got to the house she asked him in. She took out Murano tumblers for the vodka and filled them with ice. He spelled out her name in coke on the dining table. Up close the glass had tiny scratches, as though it had been scoured. You forgot the H, she said, when it was all gone. Sarah ends in a H.

Did you ever hear of tidying your room?

It isn't my room any more. I sleep in a room off the kitchen.

Do you want to go downstairs?

No. There was something vestal about the boot room. She didn't want to bring a man in there, especially this man, who was moving around the house as if he owned the place. Still, he was here, and the way he was slinking about with that townie snarl on his beardy mouth wasn't completely repulsive. She took her top off. She lay on the bed so he would have to take her jeans off, wriggle her out of her bra and knickers, tactics she had employed to amuse Davy, especially when he was fucking that bitch of an architect. She hadn't changed the sheets since Davy left. She wondered if they would smell of the woody aftershave she used to buy him but there was just a cold dustiness, like the rest of the house.

Ryan made a circle around her navel with his finger. The skin where he touched her felt like it was peeling off.

You don't remember me, do you, he said.

I don't, to be honest.

I was at the door a few times.

Are you a contractor?

He laughed. I'm in sales, I suppose, he said, and suddenly everything was clear. She remembered the story about Mattie's grandson. Davy had read it aloud one Sunday from a tabloid they didn't normally buy. A kingpin, no less, he had said as he folded the paper up. The wee knacker is a kingpin.

Davy owes you the money, she said. I've never bought drugs in my life.

That's what I thought. But you're like a Hoover, love. He turned her over and pushed her face into the mattress. She could smell Davy now.

Afterwards Ryan gave her a Valium. Before it had time to take effect she told him everything. She had persuaded Lizzie, her sister, to buy Number 7. Davy said if they got one family in, the estate would fill up in no time, it had happened with the other developments. He knocked ten grand off the price and threw in geothermal heating that never worked; they had only dug deep enough to disturb a nest of rats.

By the end Sarah was hardly sleeping, Davy beside her with his laptop on, chopping out powder in Morse-like dashes on the bedside table. Sometimes he watched porn, turning to her for rough, jittery sex that never brought either of them to climax. The sitting-room light in Number 7 stayed on through every night, and every night Sarah wanted to knock the door and say how sorry she was. One night the light went out just after three. When dawn gave up the silhouette in the fairy tree she knew it was Eoin, a steadiness about him even in death, in the pendular swing of him. Davy ripped the fairy tree from the ground the day of the funeral. He said the bad luck had already come. Sarah watched him operate the JCB and remembered who they were.

Ryan dressed at seven. He was tender towards her, pulling the sheet up to her chin and leaving a long kiss on her mouth.

I'll come back later, he said.

She went into the bathroom. She wiped her arse with the hand towel and put on a dressing gown that was hanging on the back of the door. It was white, made of brushed cotton. Downstairs, she pulled the patio door open. She lowered herself into the metal chair, letting the dew seep into her robe. Lines had begun to crackle across the yellow plaster of the houses; the roadway appeared sunken, even where there was pavement, the gardens too. Another day was breaking over Hawthorn Close.

IN SILHOUETTE

The hot pants look trampy with the platforms so you change into your yellow parallels. You pack your clutch bag with fags, a pat of powder, a tin of Vaseline. It's floppy, so you wad it with tissues to fill it out. The bag came free with a bottle of Charlie perfume you bought in the chemist's shop you're not allowed to go into because Mr Crawford, the owner, is in the DUP. A last look in the mirror. The broderie anglaise trim on your top doesn't quite reach the waistband of your trousers. Your stomach is hollow, which you like, and pale, which you don't. You go down the stairs and put your head into the sitting room. Showaddywaddy are on *Seaside Special*, wearing suits the same shade as your trousers. Cheerio, you say. Your mother pulls the edges of her cardigan together by way of an answer. You go down the driveway. The wee ones are at the stream, building a dam or demolishing one, their shrieks blowing across the fields to you. The heat has been building all day. The tarmac is spongy under your feet, sundering into oil and chips of stone, and by the time you get to the Halfway Inn the cork soles on your shoes are greasy-looking and the hair at the back of your neck is wet.

The front door is wedged open with a brick. The girls are already there, at the corner table by the jukebox, nursing jewel-coloured drinks laced with cordial. Gin and orange. Pernod and blackcurrant. Vodka and lime. You tuck your clutch high up under your arm and go to the bar.

Buy us a drink, Thady, you say. Your brother acts as if he doesn't know you're there, so you have to lean in between him and Ciaran McCann. Your top has ridden up your belly and Ciaran slants himself forward for a better look. In profile he's nearly gorgeous, but then he twists on his stool and you see the heavy lid of the eye that doesn't open. You think he's admiring you, until he sniggers. You're in no position to be laughing at anyone, Winky, you say, and he bends back over his pint. Come on, Thady, I've no money. He does this sometimes, makes you whinge stuff out of him. You're not even sure he's listening, because he has turned to look at the doorway. Everyone is looking at the doorway. It's like watching a Western, the tall silhouette against the yellow light, the face dark, in shadow. The tidy bulk of him crossing the room to the counter.

Thady must be thinking the same thing because he says Howdy, stranger.

The man smiles along the length of the bar. He's wearing a tweed sports jacket, too heavy for a summer night, and there's a spritz of sweat on his moustache. It's an evening for a few cold ones, he says, his accent going to the four corners of Ireland.

Thady puts his hand on your arm. Shandy, is it?

You reposition the bag and go across the floor to the girls. You sit at the table and they lean in and you're all talking at once. You drink fast and they dare you to ask for more. You tuck the clutch under your arm and walk to the bar, slower this time.

Buy us another one, you ask Thady.

You cost me a fortune.

Allow me, the man says.

Work away, says Thady.

When the drink is pushed at you, you hold it up at the man in thanks. *Slàinte*, he says, and you wonder if he's Scottish. He lifts a pint to his mouth. His lips are so full they hardly close.

You take some coins from the stack of change in front of your brother. You go back to the girls and put your drink on the table. Three plays, you say, and turn to the jukebox. You choose one for a laugh, one for dancing, one for the boys. As the last song finishes, Thady comes over and speaks into your ear. Go home, he says. You start to complain, swinging round to face him, but when you see the look on his face you are quiet. Night night, he says to the girls, and they clatter out ahead of you. Thady goes back to the counter. From the doorway you look at the man one last time. Now you are in silhouette, and you hope the broderie anglaise is gauzy and pure against the sunlight, and that he can see you through it. He lifts his pint at you. He sees you.

To get the free gift she has to buy two products, you explain, one skincare. You recommend the hand cream, because it's the cheapest. A wary look moves across her face as you speak, but you tone down your accent these days and she isn't sure. She drifts towards the handbags and you pack ten more of the pink velvet purses with their miniature bounty: a stubby English Rose lipstick (shade 1981), a wand of cream blusher, a canister of spray mineral water. You mist wrists with perfume, give a mini-makeover to a girl from Lingerie, clean the glass shelves. At lunchtime you take the back staircase to the staffroom. You left your bag on the windowsill in full sunlight. The smoked cheese in your sandwich has wept amber oil on to the letter from home, pages you won't open here. Yesterday's newspaper is on the table and you read it instead. There's a warship docking in Port Stanley. A pearly king and queen on Leicester Square. A street laid out for a party, bunting threaded between the lamp posts. A recipe for coronation chicken. Puffed sleeves and side fringes are in. A photograph of the silhouette man in a red and gold uniform, thick hair tamped down. A quote from his sister. *It's unbearable for my parents*. You pull the page from the paper and put it in your bag.

One of the security guards comes in. He's the man who patrols the store for unattended bags, for accents like yours. He fills a cup with water from the boiler. There are four free seats at the table but he sits in the one opposite you. He taps a sachet of dried soup into the hot water and stirs, takes a paper bag from his pocket. His sandwich is flat and damp and home-made too. He smiles at you and your face twitches with something you hope will pass for civility. You're Irish, he says. You prepare to answer, breaking up words in your mouth and reassembling them to remove the moany vowels of the place you come from, but he keeps talking. His name is Sean, *shown* the way he says it. His mum is from Carlow, which makes him eligible to play football for the Republic of Ireland. He laughs to confirm he's making a joke.

In the afternoon you shift six gift bags and sell a tube of cleavage cream to a woman in a burka with beautiful feet. He is by the swing door when you leave, walkie-talkie and polyester epaulettes swapped for a striped short-sleeved shirt with a buttoned-down collar. He acts surprised to see you, says he's going your way. He asks if you've time for a quick one – a drink, obviously. He does the laugh again. The pub is opposite the Tube station. You sit under a huge window that's misty with diesel fumes and fly spray. He asks if you'd like a Pimm's. Oh yes, you say, as though you know what it is. It comes in a dimpled beer glass with chunks of cucumber and apple in it. I don't know whether to ate it or drink it, you say, and the woman at the next table stares at you and says something into her man's ear. She is wearing a Lady Di blouse like yours.

He asks you questions as though he's reading them from a list.

Do you come from a big family?

I've an older brother and three wee sisters.

What does your brother do?

He's waiting for a job to come up.

Thady would smirk at your answer. He's three deaths away from going on hunger strike.

Sean finishes his pint in one gulp and crosses the yeasty, floral carpet to the gents. The woman at the next table is leaning in to her man, pointing at the floor where you've put your white patent-leather handbag. You pick it up, root in it, fingers moving over the greasy letter. Thady's wing is in lockdown and your mother hasn't seen him for months. You try to imagine your brother in a blanket, his hair matted with shite, but you can't picture him. You take out a lipstick and drag it slowly across your mouth, pressing your lips together when you're done. Then you use it to write four big letters across the side of your bag.

Sean appears, hoking at the waistband of his trousers. There's a light on the wall above his head and his face is grey and shiny. He takes quick, light steps to the payphone and lifts the receiver, presumably to ring the woman who made his sandwich. You turn your handbag so the couple at the next table can read it. You've written

BOMB

in shade 1981, English Rose.

It's not yet ten, and it's Saturday night, and you've been ordered home like a wee kid. Your feet are slithering in your shoes when you reach the house. You take them off in the hall and unfurl your rosy-wealed toes as you go up the stairs. The kids are in the bath, protesting the tug of a comb, the rub of a soapy cloth. You lie on your bed in your clothes. Your legs won't keep still. You close your eyes and picture the silhouette man, framed in the doorway. The table the girls were at is empty. There's no Winky, no Thady, no Mallon boy from Aughnacloy, just you on a stool with your legs crossed and a Silk Cut between your fingers, watching him. You leave him in the doorway for as long as you can bear it, let him make his way across the room to you.

Thady shakes you awake. His face is close to yours, reeking of drink. There is another smell on him, like meat or copper. You follow him to the landing. In the wan light everything is smudged, except his eyes, which are shining. He's in his stocking feet. He undresses, rolling each garment as he removes it, putting it on your waiting arms. You go into the bathroom and kneel over the tub. You've washed blood from his clothes before, slicks of afterbirth during the lambing, the bright blood of poultry. If you use hot water, it will cook and leave a stain like gravy, so you run the cold tap. You slap the jeans, the shirt, the jumper about in the flow until they are sopping, squelching them in your fists. It is a long time before the water runs clear.

You wring them as best you can and carry them out in the plastic baby bath. Thady flashes past you, his white skin almost luminous. Wait, he says. He goes into the bathroom and closes the door, opening it briefly to throw his Y-fronts on to the landing. You pick them up with a finger and thumb and go downstairs. You pull out the twin tub, fill it, turn it on, push the sodden clothes inside. In the sitting room, Thady's good shoes are propped against the brass fender on the hearth. You make a fire. You're not very good at it and use all the firelighters and a nest of willow kindling to get it going. You toss the underpants on and an oily blue flame bursts from the nylon. You poke at them until they shrink down into the embers. You can still smell shit. There's a mark on your new top. It's blood, a fine russet stain above the hem, like a feather.

Winky's at the bottom of the stairs. He's had the eye fixed. He's handsome all right, if you like the mountainy

look. Maybe you do. You put your hand on the banister.
I'll come up with you, he says. Thady's laid out on his old
bed. Someone has threaded pink rosary beads through
his fingers. Your mother is by his corpse with her handbag on her knee, the straps sitting up in two hoops as
if she's on the bus. You kiss her cheek and she shifts in
her seat. You can't remember what you're supposed to
do, so you touch Thady's shoulder and peer into his face.
They've plugged the bullet holes with putty-coloured
filler. You stay for as long as it takes to say a Hail Mary
and turn to leave the room. Winky puts his hand on the
small of your back and asks if you're OK. Yes, you say,
but that's not what comes out of your mouth. When you
can stand by yourself he brings you downstairs. Who's
that with Ciaran? someone says, and it's a second before
you know who they're talking about.

He pours you a whiskey in the kitchen and leads you
out to the back yard. You run the edge of your finger
under your eyes.

No damage done, he says.

Waterproof eyeliner, you say, and light a cigarette.

Ten years since the breakout, and they get him three
strides from the border, he says. You drop the cigarette in
the grating and go inside.

The funeral car pulls up and you get in the back with
your mother and sisters. You put your cheek against the
window and close your eyes. The wheels roll slowly over

the road and you are walking to the Halfway Inn on a summer night in your platforms, hoping to mooch a drink from your brother. Winky introduces you to his wife outside the church. She says she's sorry for your loss, her scrubbed face tensing as she takes in your painted one. At the cemetery there is a pretence of pushing back the camera crews before shots are fired over the coffin. As they crack into the air, you lower your head and adjust your sunglasses.

When you get home, someone has emptied the ashtrays, laid out trays of sandwiches. You settle your mother in her armchair and dole out tea and whiskey, wine and beer. Winky has planted himself at the bottom of the stairs. He's meeting and greeting as if he's the man of the house. You pass him with a tray, take it round the sitting room, fill it with dirty cups and saucers. In the hall you pause as if he's in your way.

Are you directing operations? you say. An eyebrow goes up and you wonder have you got away with it. He takes the tray off you and carries it to the sink. You put on pink gloves, fill the basin with hot soapy water.

I'll dry, he says, and his elbow brushes yours as he reaches across you for the tea towel. He's efficient, drying the saucers two at a time.

She has you well trained, you say. He doesn't reply.

He drives you to Aldergrove.

Some of them were talking about a ceasefire, you say.

Yeah. A few of us are back and forth to London.

You go the last ten miles in silence. At the set-off point, he flattens his fingers on the steering wheel, draws them into fists, flattens them again. You check your ticket, gather your things, prepare to tease him, but when you turn to look at him you stop. Beyond the wet window, the acetylene lamps are a shimmery orange. His face is dark. You reach a hand across and with the side of your finger you trace the hollow of his temple, the broad bone of his cheek, the line of his jaw. You get out of the car and manage not to look back.

You are early for your flight and walk around the shopping area. The cosmetic counter is grim. Last year's eyeshadow palettes, discontinued celebrity perfume. You feel sorry for the woman at the till and buy a clear mascara. Great for the eyebrows, you say. It's the first one she's ever sold. When you pass her a few minutes later with a packet of potato farls in your hand she smiles.

On the plane a stewardess hands out the next day's paper for free. There's a CCTV photograph on the front, blurred, sepia-toned. A boy leading a toddler by the hand across the concourse of a shopping centre. Thady's funeral is on page two. The headline is triumphant, but you hardly take it in, search the photo instead. It is a moment before you find yourself. You were looking for a girl in a broderie anglaise top, with a puffed-out canvas clutch bag under her arm. Winky is a row behind you, three people over. His head is turned slightly to the side. Looking at you. The next page brushes over the minor offence your brother was convicted of, lists in bullet points the ones attributed to him. The bomb that blew the wing off Mr Crawford's Rover, taking his right foot with it. The shooting dead of a UDR reservist. A post office robbery across the border, in a village by the sea. On page three there is a photograph of the silhouette man. He's young, hardly out of his teens, hair long. One of his hands is gloved and there's a kestrel perched on it. They are both looking at the camera. You fall asleep and wake with your mouth open, as the plane is landing. You pull the pages from the paper and fold them. You tuck them in the pocket in your handbag beside the bit of paper on which Winky wrote his number.

You wait for something to happen, but the days are like all the other days, slow and close. They pick you up on the roadside. You get in without a word, looking back towards the house, but you are past the bend and can't see it. You haven't been arrested, the ginger one says, as they drive you through the gates of the barracks. They bring you into a room with a blue Formica table and beige walls, although later you'll remember a greyness. They let you smoke a cigarette. The ginger one lays photographs on the table. The hump-backed bridge, the line of the McAlindens' shed behind it. The road, taken from beyond the bridge, the ivy wall of the Elizabethan fort in the right-hand corner. A beer can printed with a big-busted woman in a bikini discarded on a patch of dark, glistening grass. A tooth on tarmac, bone-white, a chunk of gristle at the root.

We already know who was in the bar, the tall one says.

What do you want me for, if you already know? you reply, and reach for your cigarettes. The ginger one takes the packet and crumbles them one by one on to the floor, like Oxo cubes.

What time did you leave? he says.

Before ten.

Who was there when you left?

You lift your shoulders. I was full, you say.

They leave the room, leave you there for an hour, two hours, the photographs still on the table. You avoid looking at the tooth, but your eyes keep going back to the beer can on the ground. The grass under it is torn up, as if it's been scrabbed by boots. There's an ache spreading across your lower back. You stand up and stretch, walk around the room, avoiding the shreds of tobacco and white paper on the floor. Your knickers are sticky.

A woman comes in. She has a Purdey hairstyle and green eyeshadow that matches the uniform. She is holding a clipboard with paper stuck to it.

I need to go to the toilet, you say.

Sit down.

I've my period.

Sit, I said. The other two come back in.

You wait for him outside Bromley South station. He appears at the top of the staircase and starts to go the wrong way, then doubles back against the crowd. His face relaxes when he sees you. You hail a black cab and tell the driver the name of the restaurant. He's carrying a dark cabin bag that he tucks behind his feet. You've booked an Italian place off the high street; you doubt he's the curry type.

They offer you a table near the window, but he points to an alcove and asks if it's free. There are broken Roman columns and plane trees painted on the walls, an alabaster bust with one bare boob on a plinth by your chair. He leans over and knocks it with his knuckles. Polystyrene, he says.

Are you complaining?

Not at all, he says – he says it like you do, not a tall – nothing like authentic Italian. Red or white?

Red makes me look like a vampire.

He passes you the wine list. You pick a Frascati that comes in a frosted bottle.

Are you hungry? he says.

Starving, you say, and order a salad. He laughs. Where do you usually stay when you're here?

I don't usually stay. We come over and back on the one day.

Fáilte go Bromley. You're in Tory heartland now.

He's careful with you. Pouring your wine, paying the bill, swinging the door to let you leave ahead of him. You walk the three streets home in the falling light, jackets over your arms. Past the fire station, the White Horse, around the corner to your house at the end of the terrace. He takes in the tiny cottage garden you planted, the pink front door.

It's like a doll's house, he says.

It's a mistress's house, you don't say. The deeds a parting gift from Sean when his wife threatened to tell their kids about you.

In the kitchen he takes a bottle wrapped in a foam sleeve from his bag and hands it to you. You take two tumblers from the dresser and go upstairs. He's three steps behind you, feet landing deliberately. You put the glasses on the nightstand with the bottle and switch on the lamps. He stands with his two arms the one length, looking around him.

You're not much of a barman, you say, and he's all apologies, making a big show of opening the bottle.

You take your evening make-up off in the bathroom, so he can't see you put on your bedtime make-up. Concealer, grey eyeliner, highlighter. Britt Ekland recommended it in a magazine article called 'Dressing up to Undress'. When you go into your room he's on the edge of your bed in his clothes. You've gone tarty with the underwear to make him feel like it's your fault. He won't look at you. You lower yourself on to his lap and start to open the buttons on his shirt. You put his hands on the cheeks of your arse but he just leaves them there. You're beginning to wonder what you can do when something occurs to you. You put your mouth to his ear, run your tongue across the lobe, say his name. You both hold your breath and then he's at you like a dog.

You called him Ciaran, obviously. He hated the nickname and anyway the eye is fixed, and you can't fuck a man you call Winky.

He passes you a brandy and you take a cigarette from the packet. There's a lighter in the nightstand beside you, you say. He pulls open the top drawer and footers around. He pulls open the second drawer. Then he swings his legs on to the floor and stares into it. He pulls the whole drawer out and sits it on his knee, flicking through the bundle of newspaper clippings.

What the fuck is this?

Put them back.

He starts to lay them out on the bed. Jesus Christ, he says. Are you right in the head?

You can't explain to him why you've been keeping them. All he can see is page after page of morbid pin-ups. He can't see what you can when you put them together.

When they let you go, your trousers are destroyed. You go into the chemist's. Crawford's daughter hands you the bag of sanitary towels, and you catch her sniggering into her hand for the benefit of the other assistant before you even turn from the counter. There's nowhere to clean yourself up. The public toilets are locked so no one can plant a bomb in them, and you can hardly go into the hotel in this state. You start walking home. A car slows, and you pull your head down into your shoulders, afraid for a moment it's them, but it's just the post van. They'll hardly lift you again, you tell yourself. You gave them what they wanted.

The wee ones have the dog pinned to the lawn, pulling a tick from him. You can hear your mother in the kitchen as you go into the hall, the soft slap of her slippers, the trickle of water over potatoes in the sink. You go into the sitting room. Thady's good shoes are still on the hearth. You take them out to the yard and scrape the dried mud and blood off them with a stone. There is something else on them, grass or hair. It's grass, you tell yourself. Just grass.

You go upstairs and run a bath. The water is tepid, and you lower yourself into it. You soap yourself and a fawn cloud billows out between your legs. There's ink on your fingers from the leaky pen they made you sign the statement with, and you take a nail brush to them, scrubbing until the pearlescent varnish starts to peel away from your nails, but the blue-black stain won't come off.

You dress yourself and go down to your mother. She slops a pie from its tin on to a Pyrex dish, spoons mounds of it on to plates. Thady appears at the back door. His face is ruddy from the sun and there's a sheaf of barley between his teeth. The wee ones come in and sit at the table and he lopes about for them like one of the Wurzels.

He takes in your wet hair. Having a bath on a Wednesday? You're good to yourself, he says.

Ha ha, you say. You sit and put a piece of meat in your mouth. It seems to get bigger as you chew.

Winky is behind him, hovering. Your mother hands them each a plate and they sit across from you.

You break up a potato with the back of your fork and lift your chin to look at him. Hiya Ciaran, you say.

Thady leans back in his chair. It's Ciaran now, is it? Must be love.

Frig off you, you say, and glance at Winky. Even his ears are red, and he lowers his head and starts eating. His sleeves are pulled down to his knuckles, cuffs skimming the thin gravy. There's a stain on his fingers. Inky black, like the stain on yours.

You thought there was little that you wanted, but you surprised yourself, have had to fold the back seat down to fit it all in. There's a box of mismatched china, a dressing table that smells of 4711 and camphor. Bone-handled cutlery, the big fish kettle your mother boiled the ham in at Christmas. The hall mirror. You'd take the fender, but your chimney is bricked up and you can't burn a coal fire in Bromley. You turn the key in the lock. You won't be back here again.

You start to get into your car but step into your walking shoes instead, rub on lip plumper. You go right at the gate. A van passes you, coming from the south, and you step up on to a hump over a ditch to get out of its path. The McAlinden place is unrecognisable, the house converted into an office, behind it a vast grey shed and the urgent hum of frightened poultry. The Elizabethan fort looks the same, ivy cloaked thickly around it. The bridge is smaller and prettier than you remember, the stones set in a pattern you never noticed as a child. You crouch on the tarmac, although the tooth is long gone, sealed in a polythene bag somewhere. Teenagers still drink here, but their tastes have changed. Buckfast, a quarter-bottle of vodka. An empty Kettle Chips bag. You thought you'd find an imprint, a trace, but there is nothing. Just a pretty hump-backed bridge, lush fields, an ivy-clad ruin.

You walk back to the house, change into your heels. You open the windows as you turn left out of the driveway, wanting to fill the car with the damp scent of the land. A gust of wind and the rank chicken smell is there instead.

A new bar and restaurant stands on the site where the Halfway Inn was, the entrance at the side. The car park is filling with the Sunday lunch crowd. You take a table by the front window, thinking it is where the jukebox once was, but the new building is further back from the road than the original and you aren't sure. You were supposed to arrive first so Ciaran could saunter in and act surprised to see you. He's at the bar with a whiskey cupped in his palm.

He crosses the room and sits heavily in front of you.

You were meant to be here half an hour ago.

I went for a walk.

Where to?

Down to the bridge.

Fuck's sake.

A waitress comes to take your order. Her eyebrows are thinner than her eyeliner, and a silver stud flashes on her tongue as she recites the specials. You ask her for a salad and fizzy water. He orders another whiskey.

You should eat something.

I'm not hungry.

Herself'll have the roast on, I suppose.

He watches you eat. He watches you all the time now, as though you're liable to do anything. When he gets up to pay the bill you find yourself pacing out the floor, trying to walk where the silhouette man walked, but you don't know where the front door was, or the bar. He turns from the till and hisses at you.

The hell are you at?

I shake leaves from a bag on to a plate, tip pieces of cooked chicken over them. I bring it to the couch and switch on the television, go into Recordings, press play. The camera spans the field, taking in the fort, the chicken farm, the hump-backed bridge. The sky is thick and white. The reporter is in front of the bar and grill where the Halfway Inn once stood. He points at the corner of the car park. Forty years ago, he says. The photographs, then. The silhouette man in his red and gold uniform against a backdrop of painted trees and columns. Him again, a beret pulled down to the tips of his ears, surrounded by women on a street strewn with masonry. Thady's body on a wet road, feet turned out, a piece of cloth over his head and shoulders.

There's a man in an empty room, his head turned a little to the left, lit dimly from behind. The line of his jaw is heavy, thickened by drink. He starts to speak, but it's not his voice and the actor is too young for the words. *There were four of us left in the bar. Thady, Mallon, the soldier and me. We followed him out to the car park and had a go at him. It took three of us to get him into the car. We went at him again by the bridge, for hours.* He pauses, takes a drink of water. *He told us nothing. He was the bravest man I ever met. A fucking headcase.* He lifts a hand to his forehead, and I can see it, just for a second. The slightest droop of the eye.

I light a scented candle in the hall and switch on the UV lamp on the table in my parlour. I lay out a bowl of warm water, phials of shellac, polish, glitter. My two o'clock appointment arrives, three minutes early. She is my age, with a glossy forehead and a leathery chest. I rub off the old paint and lower her hands into the basin, holding them in mine as I work back the cuticles. She chooses a burnt-orange colour that she saw in a magazine. I apply it in thin layers, drying each coat under the lamp. The blue light gives up age spots and ropey veins. She watches, a look of fear in her eyes. She tells me a secret. They always do.

HUNTER-GATHERERS

The hare wasn't ten feet away, the closest he had ever come. He was bigger than Siobhán had realised, legs stocky, white tail cartoon-fluffy. In spite of his heft there was a lightness in the way he flumped about. He paused, held himself very straight. Siobhán fancied he was looking at her, though it was unlikely he could see her. The back garden was shaded by a dense grove of sally trees and the winter light was thin.

He's there again now. You told me they only come out at night.

You'll often see them at this time, or in the evening, said Sid. He leaned into her back, pushing her against the sink, and banged the kitchen window with the heel of his hand. In a single leap the hare cleared the beech saplings Sid had planted in the autumn, ears making a V-sign, and took off in the direction of the house.

You frightened him.

Cheeky bastard's after tipping my new hedge.

He's beautiful.

He? It, you mean. The thing's a pest, Townie. He lifted her hair and scraped his chin across the nape of her neck.

Stop.

You know you want to.

You're not funny. The Pajero puttered to a halt outside. I'm gone, she said and made for the bedroom. Sid caught her wrist.

Say hello at least, don't be ignorant.

Siobhán pulled her fleece across herself, wishing she had put a bra on. Peadar let himself in and stood on the hearthrug in his boots. He and Sid wore identical camouflage hunting jackets in shades of russet and olive and brown. It was the last day of the shooting season. Siobhán and Sid rented the gate lodge of the Fitzroy family's country estate, which was known for its wild game and salmon. Peadar was the gamekeeper, Sid one of the beaters. They had been friends since school.

Well, Peadar said. In one hand he had a bottle of *poitín* that he gave to Sid. Two dead birds dangled from the other. He offered them to Siobhán with a sidelong look at Sid. Both men laughed when she shrank back. Peadar followed Sid to the kitchen. He had parked so close to the porch diesel fumes were panting into the sitting room. Siobhán went to shut the front door. Dogs were yelping from the back of the jeep, and a slight girl was in the passenger seat, limp brown hair framing a small face. She was wearing a waxed jacket that was too big for her and a man's tweed cap. Siobhán gestured at her to come in. The girl raised an eyebrow and a shoulder and looked the other way. Siobhán left the door ajar and went inside.

Who's the young one? she asked Peadar.

Rachael. The girlfriend's daughter.

Should she not be in school?

She's in Transition Year. She was at me to bring her dog with her to train it.

Bring her in, sure.

She's grand where she is.

I'll be late this evening, said Sid. He kissed Siobhán's forehead. Champagne and canapés with Lady Muck, and a few scoops in Dolan's.

Well for you, Siobhán said, backing towards the bedroom. The previous morning Peadar had kissed her goodbye too. And sniffed her. *Like a dog*, she had told Sid. Sid had just laughed.

Peadar's a hunter. A man's man.

He's a creep, Sid.

She went to the porch and watched them leave. Rachael answered her wave with a stare. Peadar reversed on to the lawn and took off towards the house; on his spare-wheel cover there was a faded silhouette of two rhinos, one mounting the other from behind. For a second the lake glinted beyond them, a silver line in the distance. She and Sid had come to live here the previous Easter, yet she was still moved by the place, by the pastoral sweep of parkland that stretched to the right of the cottage, how it changed every day. This morning the copse of oaks before the bend was crisp with hoarfrost.

She ladled water from the rain barrel at the side of the house and sloshed it around the cyclamen she had potted on either side of the door, taking care not to let the icy water touch the leaves. She thought the lodge beautiful. It was a scaled-down model of the house, generous in width yet one room deep, with four columns holding up a miniature portico. Vanessa Fitzroy had had it painted in Farrow and Ball colours and hung Liberty print curtains. Now that it was winter, white mould bloomed in the walls and several times a day Siobhán blotted condensation from the windows with an old towel.

She went back inside and through to the kitchen. The dead birds were on the draining board. She flipped one of them over with the end of a wooden spoon, saw a flash of jade at the wing tip, the tiny nib of its beak. It was a teal. She put the kettle on for a cup of tea. Sid said they should buy local produce, and was keen for her to drink a herbal infusion made by an English woman who was living off the grid near Drumshanbo. Siobhán thought it smelled like silage, that Barry's of Cork was local enough.

Sid had bought books online about self-sufficiency and foraging. For the month of February they would eat only wild food. It would be a lean month for plants and leaves, he said, but they would manage. At the summer's end they gathered stuff she hadn't known was edible and preserved it. The freezer was full of nettle puree and wild garlic pesto. On the kitchen dresser there were jars of pickled alexanders and rowan jelly, bottles of sloe gin. There were powdered puffballs that Sid wanted her to use instead of stock cubes, pots of magic mushrooms suspended in honey. She didn't trust Sid with the mushrooms. Once he had brought home a deadly Amanita that was seething with worms. Later they had pegged chanterelles and hedgehog fungus to flimsy makeshift clothes lines that criss-crossed the spare bedroom. The first batch had rotted in the damp. The next was a success because they had plugged an electric heater in the room for a week.

Siobhán put on a green tweed coat and mauve mohair scarf, and fur-lined ankle boots. Her mad-ould-one outfit, according to Sid. She drove the three miles into town and parked at the back of SuperValu. Christmas lights, disconnected and dribbling rust, were still swinging over Main Street as she crossed it. The library was housed in a former Protestant church that sat back from the footpath. The children's books were just inside the door on the left. A group of small girls were in a ring on the floor with their teacher, weaving Brigid's crosses from rushes to mark the start of spring the next day. The cross was said to guard a home from evil, fire and hunger. Siobhán might pick rushes at the lakeshore later, see if she remembered how to make one. Maybe it would guard them against visits from Peadar. She returned her books and asked the assistant where she could find information about hares.

Fifth from the left, third shelf down, said a high, quick voice behind her. She turned to see who had spoken. It was Xavier Looby. He was sitting in the study area, two large rectangular tables pushed together. Opposite him, two schoolgirls were giggling over the 'Out and About' pages of the *Sligo Champion*. To their right a young black man was filling in a form.

Soon she found what she wanted. All the chairs were taken except the one next to Xavier Looby. She sat down. Xavier had been in Sid's class in school. Siobhán had often seen him walking the roads far from his bungalow on the edge of the town. His lawn swayed knee high, and children threw stones at his windows. Today he was wearing a sou'wester and shiny golf jacket. One leg of his tracksuit bottoms was torn from inside the thigh to below the knee. His leg was pale and shapely. Four thick biographies of Elizabeth I were stacked in front of him. Siobhán opened an old *Encyclopaedia of Wildlife* and found the right chapter. It had photographs of mountain hares, European hares, American jackrabbits.

Xavier Looby cleared his throat. Siobhán turned to look at him. *Lepus timidus hibernicus*, he said, eyes bright behind the greasy lenses of his glasses, the Latin words grave and glottal, like an incantation. He told her that the Irish hare doesn't turn white in winter. He told her the Druids thought the hare was a manifestation of the moon goddess Eostre, who we named Easter after. He told her that Boudicca once released a hare from her skirt before a battle, and that the hare was on the old Irish threepenny bit. He told her it was thought that the young males boxed out of rivalry, but that scientists now know the females box the males away when they don't want to copulate. He told her the ancient Irish believed hares were shape-shifters, related to the sídhe, because a hare screams like a woman when it's hurt. Around the table, the girls had stopped giggling, the young man had put down his pen.

A hare comes into my garden, Siobhán said. I can't wait to see it leaping round the place in March. But the spell was broken and Xavier Looby was quiet. He folded back into himself and picked at a long thread on the open seam of his bottoms. As she went to put back the books, he reached forward and tapped one of them with yellowy fingers. She borrowed it at the desk as she was leaving.

She went into SuperValu. Her shopping list was short, just biscuits, nuts and chocolate to add to her secret cache. On her way to pay, a woman stopped her.

Well, stranger. Nicola Leyden was smiling, baring teeth so white they seemed to luminesce. She was wearing a black and pink kimono with her name on it. Her beauty clinic was above the supermarket. What are you up to?

I was in the library.

Weirdo. Do me a favour, will you? She took ten euros from her pocket. Would you ever buy me a box of super plus and a bag of towels?

Do you not want to get the discount on them?

Alan Fox is on today. I'd die if he knew.

You have a kid to him. He must know you have periods.

His wife let herself go. I want to keep the bit of glamour going.

As Siobhán approached the checkouts, Alan Fox disappeared through a door marked PRIVATE. The doughy boy behind the counter looked miserably at the contents of her basket and had to scan the tampons three times before the till accepted the code. Siobhán wondered if Sid would like her to spend her periods squatting in a hedgerow with a wad of dock leaves, like Queen Maeve. She sniggered, out loud. The boy fled, knocking against a display of Valentine's Day cards.

Nicola was waiting at the back of the shop. How's life with Bear Grylls? she said, tucking her supplies under her arm.

Grand. Last day of the shooting season today.

You're like death.

Thanks.

Come up to me later and I'll do your tan.

You'd want to be lightening yours. You're the colour of a brick.

I couldn't give two shites. Fake is fake. Have you time for a cup of coffee?

Siobhán wanted to go home and read the library book before Sid came back. She made an excuse.

Xavier Looby was by the bottle bank, flicking curry chips into his mouth with his fingers, hunched and feral again away from the library. She paused to say hello but he didn't lift his head. Sid said Xavier Looby had been persecuted at school. Siobhán wondered if Sid had been one of his tormentors. Before the Garda station closed, Sid's father had been the sergeant. Sid, the copper's kid. Considering he knew everything that went on in the town, Sergeant Hennigan had been oblivious to his son's drug peddling, to his fighting and thieving. Still, surely Sid would have hunted more artful prey than Xavier?

On the way home she called in to Great Gas for diesel. She bought a chicken fillet roll and a Diet Coke as well. Tomorrow they would begin living off the land and the prospect depressed her. When she pulled up at the lodge, she could hear shots in the distance. Sid had been home. He had left a change of clothes across the back of the couch. She brought them out to the car and drove towards the house; otherwise Peadar would drive him home to get them, and Sid would ask him in again.

It was only three but already the sky had dimmed. To the left of the house the grey lake lapped against the reeds and rushes. The gunfire was getting louder as she turned right towards the coach yard. Jeeps and trailers and small white vans were parked along the lane, the Pajero at the end. She left her car around the corner and followed the shouts and shots and barks.

They were in an open space in the field that bordered the hazel wood. Ten men were standing at posts positioned at regular intervals in a row. Peadar and Sid and the other beaters were behind them, by a bosk of holly. Suddenly pheasants flew up, a flock of eleven or twelve. They seemed to Siobhán to be disorientated, flapping weakly. There was a shout and the men at the posts had time to raise their guns and fire. Six birds fell and the dogs retrieved them. A seventh bird, which Siobhán had seen take a hit, flew towards the lake, sinking into the horizon as it struggled. She waited for one of the beaters to send a dog after it, but they just stood there. She started to walk towards Sid. She hadn't thought to put her wellingtons on, so the heavy ground sucked at her heels.

One of the birds is wounded. You need to bring a dog over to the lake, she told Sid. Peadar whispered something to Rachael that made her smirk.

They can fly half a mile like that. We'd never find it, said Sid, without looking at her. She pushed his clothes at him and went back to the car, her righteous gait hampered by the wrong footwear. On the lane she had to brake hard to avoid hitting a stick-legged bird with no plumage, just tufts of sparse down. Vanessa Fitzroy was behind it, swathed in cashmere the colour of heather, swinging a shillelagh. Siobhán opened the window.

What the fuck is that? she said.

Henrietta is a rescue hen, poor thing.

They're slaughtering healthy birds up there. Why would you rescue that yoke?

Bridie, the cleaning lady, had told Siobhán that Vanessa spent her days lying on the couch eating chicken nuggets and FaceTiming her friends in Cape Town. Vanessa had invited Siobhán to the house for coffee a few times but, by the look on her face, was unlikely to ask her again. Siobhán closed her window and drove too fast towards the cottage, wanting to get away, too angry to stop by the lake for reeds.

Inside, she lit a fire. The twigs and shoots Sid gathered were always damp so the room grew smoky. At the sink she washed the breakfast dishes, trying not to look at the dead birds or think about the wounded pheasant flitting away from the men's guns. Sid's copy of *Food for Free* was propped open on the windowsill. He had bought it a few months earlier and already it had begun to fade and curl. It occurred to Siobhán he had aged it on purpose. She made another cup of tea and brought it to the sitting room. The fire had caught and was spitting brightly. She took out the book Xavier Looby had recommended. It was an anthology of folk tales collected by Yeats, with art nouveau illustrations. She began to read a story called 'Bewitched Butter', about a magical cow in Donegal.

Sid came home after seven, with Peadar and Rachael. He hadn't changed his clothes.

Drink! he said. Siobhán followed him to the kitchen.

What's the story?

Relax. They're only here for one or two.

What age is that girl?

Fuck knows. Will you have one? He waved the *poitín* at her. Chill, will you? he said when she didn't answer. He brought the bottle to the sitting room with three shot glasses. Rachael was on the couch beside Peadar, flushed. Siobhán forced a smile.

How did you get on today, Rachael?

It was cool.

I was thinking about that poor pheasant.

There was a rake of them hit like that, said Rachael, raising the eyebrow and shoulder again.

Sid glanced at Peadar. That ould Yank only half hit most of his, the fucking eejit. All the right gear and he couldn't kill shite. The others laughed.

Siobhán took her book and went down the hall. Sid would tell her later it was all her own fault, that she wasn't on the same buzz as them. She lay on top of the bed and tried to ignore Sid flicking through tracks on his iPod, Peadar's voice, slow and careful, Rachael's sudden laughter. Siobhán knew Sid would settle on 'Kashmir'. Still, when she heard the opening bars she felt a lurch of something, of fury almost, that surprised her. She would avoid him for the rest of the evening, have a long bath when the others left. The volume went up a couple of notches, bass thudding in the walls. If she asked them to turn it down there would be a scene, so she stayed in the bedroom, the book in her lap unopened, and waited.

Outside in the garden the sensor light came on. The music stopped, truncating a guitar's long *waang*; there was a clattering of feet and furniture. A car door slammed, barking dogs were hushed, feet crossed the oak boards again. For a few seconds all was quiet, then from beyond the bedroom window a whisper: Sid's voice, thick with drink.

Go *on*.

A brisk click, then Peadar said, Now.

A single shot sounded, followed by a woman's scream: long, dreadful, full of anguish. Something had happened to Rachael. At first Siobhán just sat on the edge of the bed, her mind skittering. She went to the window, wiped her sleeve across the condensation, but could see nothing. Another shot, and this time the cry was a shriek that waned to a desolate gurgle. What had they done? Siobhán left the bedroom and went along the hall. The sitting room was empty, a draught coming from the open back door. Outside a crest of gun smoke turned in the air and near the beech hedging the grass was tarry. The sensor light went off and, for a moment, Siobhán couldn't see. She heard a murmur, a gasp, a tiny giggle. Peadar and Rachael were beyond the kitchen windowsill. Peadar's right hand was flat on the wall, his other on the handle of the gun he was twirling into the ground, the girl looking up at him through a straggle of hair. They didn't see her. Where was Sid?

Siobhán went back inside. The house reeked of shit and iron and offal. She sidestepped the dark blobs on the floor and followed them to the kitchen. Sid turned from the sink. The hare was on the draining board, ears flopping backwards, once-white belly muddied. He seemed huge, hind legs reaching beyond the kettle. There was a treacly hole at the front of his head, his eyes were hazel and still. Sid took a hunting knife from his pocket and drew it across the animal's throat, turning him quickly to catch the blood in a jug. Siobhán stumbled out the front door and steadied herself against one of the pillars. He followed her, the knife in his hand.

You killed him.

Her. It was a female. I told you this morning we'd have to get rid of it.

Jesus Christ. You shot her and brought her into the kitchen?

Rachael shot it.

Rachael?

Hit it first time. Clean. Never saw anything like it for a young one.

She has drink on her and you gave her a gun. She's a child.

Peadar said it was OK.

Are you mental? What is even going on with Peadar and that girl? Is he planning on driving her home?

He's had fuck all to drink.

Get them out of here or I will.

Fuck's sake.

Fine. Siobhán went out the back. Peadar and Rachael stepped from the shadows as the light came on.

I'm sure your mother will be wondering where you are, Rachael, she said. Peadar nodded at the girl and she went to the jeep without a word.

Siobhán went to the bedroom and closed the door. She thought of the hare, how it had taken six or seven visits for her to come as close as she had that morning, how she had come back that evening. She pictured her near the kitchen window, pert yet timorous, eyes widening in the glare of the light. She picked up the book. It opened on the first page of a story that Yeats had written. She could hardly believe the illustration: the close thicket of trees, the candyfloss tail and meaty hind legs clearing a hedge, ears in a V-sign. She read the story three times. It was about a man who is led astray on a hunt by a mysterious hare and is never seen again.

Sid opened the door and stood slack-shouldered at the foot of the bed, in a stance of remorse.

Look, I cleared it all up.

I don't want to talk to you.

Things die.

She didn't just die.

We're in the countryside. I thought you got it.

I thought you weren't a prick. The book was still open in her lap.

Sid knelt on the floor beside Siobhán. He put a strand of hair behind her ear and dragged a thumb across her cheek. His hand smelled like slaughter.

WOLF POINT

The statue stood in a clearing. It was a wood nymph, lifelike yet diminutive, the height of an adolescent girl. A dappling of sunlight was flickering over her, the long light of late summer. Tendrils of ivy crowned her head. Fronds of maidenhair and lady fern were fanned out behind her, like the backdrop for a Victorian daguerreotype. She was leaning forward at the waist, left hip cocked, right arm outstretched, as if beckoning him into the place where the trees were deepest. Peter kicked through briars and thistles to reach her. Up close she looked sickly, a film of algae discolouring the marble. Peter put his hand in hers – it was big and coarse in comparison. He drew it away.

The wood had been part of an estate that had once stretched along the west shore of the lake from the edge of the town to the Leitrim border. An heir to the house had planted it to enchant his young English bride, a teenage girl who had been sent to this corner of Connaught, part of a deal to save the estate after the famine. He had filled the wood with follies and ornaments that Peter came across from time to time when he was working.

A brick-built doll's house, broken windows glittering on the forest floor. A wrought-iron birdcage, big enough to hold a person. This marble woman-child. Over the centuries they had been swallowed by the woodland. Peter found it unsettling when they were revealed to him. He left the clearing and went back to his van along the path that rimmed Half Moon Bay.

When he got to the house, Clary was sitting on the gatepost. She was in her pyjamas, feet flexed to keep on her polka-dot wellingtons, a plastic tiara holding her hair off her face. Peter opened the passenger window.

Can I take you some place, madam?

Will you let me drive?

He nodded. She came in the window headfirst and climbed on to his knee. She put her left hand on his on the gearstick. Her fingers were cold. Peter worked the pedals while she creaked through the gears, letting her think she was driving all by herself. At the top of the driveway she pulled the steering wheel hard. The wing mirror scraped against the porch. She drew in her shoulders and glanced back at him, tears collecting in her eyes. He straightened the van up and turned off the engine.

You might need to do the Driver Theory Test, he said. He carried her into the house. It was as he'd left it a couple of hours earlier, except for a saucepan of water on the stove, dead matches scattered among the gas jets. He sat her on the settee, tucking a throw around her.

I'm hungry, Daddy.

I'll put us on a bit of breakfast. He filled the kettle and lit a fire under three eggs.

The curtains were still drawn in the bedroom. Emma was on her side, the duvet bunched down at her waist. She looked like herself when she was sleeping. Her lips were parted, and a couple of buttons on her nightshirt had opened. One breast was exposed, full and white.

Emma. He shook her shoulder. Emma. You said you'd get up.

He watched her try to reach out of the torpor she was in, arms pushing from their sockets, legs stretching. She turned from the wall and looked at him, dread at the prospect of a new day moving over her face.

What time is it?

It's after ten. The child was by the gate again, he said, passing her a pint of water from the bedside table.

Emma took a long drink. Jesus, she said.

She tried to make herself breakfast.

Emma lay back on the pillow. Please don't be cross.

I've a bit of food on now.

When the eggs were sitting in their cups, Clary capped them with cosies, tiny rainbow-striped beanie hats that Emma had knitted the month she didn't sleep. Peter spread their toast with butter and Marmite.

Cut them in soldiers, like Mummy does, said Clary. She said it the way Emma would, putting the Bristol r in soldiers. Peter took a tray from the top of the fridge and Clary covered it with a linen cloth that Emma had bought at a jumble sale in the Methodist Hall. It was edged with embroidered bluebells and looped with tea stains. She laid out her mother's breakfast and Peter brought it to the bedroom.

Emma had made an attempt at sitting up. She was sloped against two pillows. Peter smoothed the bedspread and put the tray down beside her. Lovely, she said, without looking at it.

You might get up today, he said, and left the room.

Clary had set three places at the table. She did it for every meal. He hadn't told her what happened at the lake that day, but he sometimes wondered if she knew. The neighbour who made the 999 call said he'd keep it to himself, but Peter could almost hear him telling the story. *She walked into the water, the clothes still on her. Walked in and lay down.*

Clary held a mug out.

You're like a wee granny, with your cups of tea, said Peter. She put in her own milk and sugar. He sliced the top off her egg and watched her test it with the first soldier.

Top banana, she said.

He ran water over the dishes in the sink while Clary got herself dressed. The J Cloth in the basin was warm with bacteria. He slung it into the bin and looked around. The place was dirty. He tried to find time for cleaning after work, but the evenings slid away from him. On nights when Emma joined them in front of the television, crumpled in on herself in a corner of the couch, he and Clary didn't leave her side. They brought her mugs of tea and fresh ashtrays, glasses of water for washing down tablets. By the time he read to Clary and cleared up after dinner, all he managed was a spliff at the back door and some sleep.

In the bedroom, Emma was lying down again. She had eaten nothing.

I'll bring her with me, said Peter. You might put clothes on you. Have a shower or something. He kissed her. Her mouth was gluey, metallic, a side effect from the new medication. Each one did something different to her. She said the best had been the one that gave her spontaneous orgasms, squirts of ecstasy that came without warning in Spar or at the clothes line. The worst had been lithium. She said it was like being inside one of the bubbles Clary loved to blow, wobbling on the end of a plastic wand and waiting for the glassy membrane around her to burst. She had begun to look puffy too, but Peter hadn't told her so.

Clary came back wearing jeans and a floaty halter-necked top she had demanded he buy her in Penneys. It'll be too cold by the lake, he said. She scowled until they found a compromise; she put a jumper on under it.

They made a picnic. Clary pushed ham into floury rolls and packed them in a Tupperware tub with a couple of apples. Peter filled a flask with tea, and jam jars with milk and sugar. There was chocolate and a bottle of orange in the van. He strapped Clary into the passenger seat.

To the Fairy Grove! she said. The tiara was over one eye.

The wood was less than a mile away from the house, close enough for Peter to go back and forth to check on Clary. Often McTiernan showed up, trying to catch him out. He had arrived one morning with an inspector from Dublin to check for the fungus that was killing ash trees in England. It had reached the south-east, come over on the B&I boat, he said; it wouldn't take much for it to spread this far. Clary had been gathering flowers and appeared with an armload of cow parsley and columbine, beaming as though she had just won the Eurovision Song Contest. She had waited for the men to speak to her, her face creasing with indignation when it became clear she was being ignored. Later, McTiernan had given him a warning about bringing his daughter to work.

Since then, Peter had begun taking Clary to Wolf Point, a narrow promontory that fingered the lake. It was almost a mile from the car park, and McTiernan was too lazy to walk the distance. The Forestry had a yard and lock-up shed at the entrance to the wood. Peter parked so McTiernan would see his van from the road.

He loaded a couple of bags of gravel on to the tractor, as if he was going to repair one of the paths, while Clary took what they needed from the van and hunkered down on the floor of the cab at his feet. They juddered along the lakeshore path, Peter raising a finger in salute at the walkers and joggers he passed. No one seemed to notice there was a child with him.

He pulled in behind a thicket of holly and spindle. Clary took his hand and jumped down. He threw a tartan rug around her shoulders and followed her into the trees. Untainted by dog piss or the tramp of hiking boots, Wolf Point was lush. Each season brought something on: primroses and wood anemones in spring, amethyst deceivers and penny buns in autumn. Even winter had a bounty: a cluster of berries the birds had missed, lime-white lichen through freezing fog. Above them, the ash trees had begun to turn, the black fruit wizened, the leaves yellowed. They were always the first trees to fade, a herald of the end of summer.

Clary swiped at long grasses with the cape she had made of the tartan blanket. She stopped to show him broomrape, a rare plant that could not take in light and lived as a parasite on the roots of ivy. The ruin of a bower was part-covered by bracken, its two rooms sunken and marked in stone furred with bright moss. It wasn't much bigger than the doll's house that had been built for the lady. He feared Clary would fall in but she stumbled on, hauling the blanket back over her shoulder as it slid off. When they came to the clearing she turned to him.

Can I put our stuff on Mummy's chair? She was frowning. He could see she felt disloyal for asking, for writing her mother out of the day. Later she would do what he did, talk about Emma as if she had been with them, try to write her back in.

Two years ago a storm had taken down an old ash. As it fell it clipped two more, splitting one to the roots, leaving the other swaying like a drunk. He took a chainsaw to them. Emma came later with Clary. He was about to complain that the child had been kept home from play-school again, but as always found himself mesmerised by Emma's enthusiasm. A fairy grove! Just for the three of them! The stumps were a sorry sight, but not for long. She had got him to carve the two largest into thrones. The last would be a toadstool, she said, because any fairy ring worth its salt had a toadstool. She took his pocket knife and began to dig words from each one. *Ivy killed me. Rhoda killed me.* She carved *Little Nymph* on the toadstool.

Will we have the picnic now?

You're only after your breakfast.

But I'm hungry. She opened the chocolate bar. You should have bought a minty Aero, she said and took a bite.

Give it to me so.

He tried to snatch it off her. She pushed the rest of the bar into her mouth, where it bulged in her cheek. She looked uncomfortable and triumphant at once. Above them, ivy-clad ash and sycamore creaked in the wind that was coming off the lake. Ivy stockings, Emma called them. Once she named a thing, it became more than it had been. Like the night he met her.

He had been at the bar in Heneghan's, sitting three stools away from the fire like he always did. She came in and ordered a cider. Her hair was wiry and unkempt, her complexion mottled. When the glass was put in front of her she counted out coins. Her fingernails were dirtier than his. There was a table quiz on for the local GAA club. They were shamed into making a team, just the two of them. He paid the twenty quid. She worked for an English organic farmer called Mervyn just over the Leitrim border. The advert had said there would be several workers, but she was the only one. Peter watched Emma as she talked. As it got warmer she pulled her jumper off. She wasn't wearing a bra under her top. She noticed that he had noticed. He felt colour rise in his face. She smirked.

So what do you do? she said.

I work for the Forestry.

You're a woodsman! Peter the Woodsman. Like a Russian fairy tale. And after that he was.

A couple of days later Emma appeared when he was working. He knew every stand and thicket in the wood but didn't feel they were his until he walked the paths with her. She had a name for each grass and reed, each herb and flower. They sat on a bench by Half Moon Bay as a gale came up. They shared a cigarette and watched a mallard and her young try to tread the roily water that was slapping them towards the shore. When the last car had left Emma disappeared into a rhododendron and came out with an old bicycle. It didn't have reflectors, let alone a light, and she was staying six miles away. Peter ignored her protests and lifted the bike into the van.

The organic farm was not what he expected. The original cottage had been added to, a grass-roofed structure, clearly architect-designed, growing from the side that overlooked a glen. Mervyn came out and watched them from the doorway. He was slight and swarthy, hair slicked into a thin grey ponytail.

Hiya! called Emma. Mervyn scarcely nodded in reply.

The head on that, said Peter.

She came into Heneghan's a few days later. Mervyn's wife had gone to Norwich to visit her mother.

That fella has a wife? said Peter, to make her laugh. She hooked her thumbs into the opposite cuffs and pulled her sleeves over her hands. Mervyn had drunk a batch of home brew and banged at the door of her caravan. She would have to find something else. A different job, a new place to live. She couldn't go back to Bristol. She spoke without looking at him. She stood up, leaving half her drink. He watched her go out the door and felt he wanted to tell her something. He just didn't know what. He threw his pint into himself and followed her. She was getting on the bike.

You'll get knocked down, he said. She began to cry. She could stay with him, he said. There was a spare room. He wouldn't go near her. As they went into his house, he caught a glimpse of them in the hall mirror. Beside him, she looked like a girl.

I'm forty-three, he said.

She was there a fortnight before she came into his bed. I'm twenty-two, she said, if that's what's worrying you. When McTiernan called to the door the next morning to ask why he wasn't at work, Peter the Woodsman couldn't keep the smile from his face.

Clary pulled his sleeve. Let me see the wind rush, she said.

You can't see it. You can only hear it.

How will I hear it?

You'd want to stay quiet, for a start.

Lift me up high.

He hoisted her on to his shoulders. A gust of wind came, keen and cool, that made Clary gasp. Above them leaves bristled, a trickling sound like water washing rocks. She stayed there for a few minutes, quiet in the stillness between each gust, jerking with a start when the wind gathered the air and sent it whistling past them.

Let me down, she said. I'm starving.

You couldn't be. She reached for the bottle of orange. He took it and held it high. If you're hungry have a roll.

Shall we have a cup of tea, then?

He watched Clary with the flask, the enamel mugs. At five she was matronly, attempting the domesticity her mother couldn't manage. She could have burned herself earlier, or left the gas on. Emma wasn't fit to look after her. He didn't know what to do.

He had to try hard to remember the beginning. Emma's appearance seemed like sorcery now. She wasn't there, and then she was, without preamble or courtship. He hadn't realised what a bachelor he had become until they ate together. He had to train himself not to lower his head to the plate and clear it. They lit a fire every night, even in summer. She put on music, plaintive songs by English girls who looked like her, and passed him neatly rolled joints. Even now he lay awake long after she was asleep, aware of her beside him. Of her mad hair that tangled around his watch and found its way into his mouth. Of her legs, crossed at the ankles, that tethered his feet. Of the grubby purity she brought to his life.

Clary was walking, had a few words, when it started. He came home one evening to find her alone in the house, vomit-drenched and whimpering in her cot. Emma was by the lake, cross-legged on the jetty his grandfather had made. He carried her home. As Clary toddled around the sitting room, Emma lay on the couch and didn't appear to notice she was there. The next day she seemed herself again. She didn't know what had come over her.

I'm still hungry, Daddy.

You'd wear a man down.

She laid out the picnic on Emma's throne. He opened the bottle of orange for her, and licked drips off the back of his hand.

I left a roll for Mummy.

You're a wee star.

Clary took a bite. Everything tastes better outdoors, she said. It was something her mother might have said.

When they had finished, Clary tidied up. She took off her tiara and pulled a length of ivy from the base of a sycamore, winding it around and around the plastic until it was an arc of lush green. Peter placed it on her head and she smiled up at him. The day Emma walked into the lake he had been in this place, a smell of raw wood still in the air from the three newly hewn seats. He had thought the sound was the engine of a boat, or farm machinery on the far shore; then the helicopter had paused above him and crossed Half Moon Bay. Through the rushes he had seen the winch sweep the water at the foot of his own garden. When he got to the hospital Emma was asleep, a leaden chemical slumber. He sat by her bed and waited. When she came around and realised she had been rescued she had to be sedated again.

Clary was in the centre of the fairy grove, the blanket draped over one shoulder, the ivy crown bedded into the blonde hair she refused to brush. The wind rushed again and they both looked up. A single leaf had fallen from the tallest ash and was caught on the wind. For a moment it looked as if it might be carried away, but it began to drift towards them, spinning, dancing. Clary reached out her arm and cupped her hand. The leaf tumbled in the air, righted itself, and floated on downwards. It seemed to pause before it landed on her open palm, dry and gauzy. The season was turning.

BELLADONNA

She sits in the front row now, among the drips she used to persecute. They've taken to smiling at her, eyes soft with pity. Róisín looks through them. She's not ready to join their tragic ranks. It's bearable when she stays quiet, but sometimes in classes she enjoys, English or history, she forgets herself and puts her hand up to answer a question. She can hear them then, the girls who used to be her friends, whispering and laughing at the back.

Breaktime and lunchtime are the worst, when she has to walk past them to get out the door. Most days at eleven she locks herself into one of the toilet cubicles. Not the furthest one, because someone has scraped her name on to the back of the door with the letters RIP under it. At one she usually goes to the library.

Today Mr Butler is on duty. He's smoking a cigarette out the window. When he sees Róisín, he flicks it on to the tennis court below and crosses to the desk, pumping Gold Spot into his mouth. He gives her a mustardy smile and starts to flip through a long box of cards. She goes to the fiction shelves. She's read all the ones she likes the look of. She can hear the squeak of his brown Bobcats, feels his breath on her hair. He's holding a skinny book with a blue cover. You might like this, he says, since you're from the north. He asks if she'd like to hear one of the poems. It feels like such a long time since anyone except her mother has spoken to her she says yes.

When Sister Margaret Mary comes in, Róisín is sitting on a table, where Mr Butler said she might be most comfortable. He's a foot away, on a chair, reading in the poety voice that makes everyone snigger in class. It isn't until he jumps up and holds the book over his crotch that Róisín realises what's going on. For the rest of the afternoon she draws her hair across her face like curtains and tries not to think about the bulge in the front of Mr Butler's trousers, or the way the nun looked at her.

The house is quiet. Róisín's mother is on a week of nights and still in bed. Róisín lays her schoolbooks out on the table in the front room. A removal van slows and stops outside the bungalow across the road. Two men wearing thick gloves begin to unload it. Soon tea chests and antique furniture are spread across the garden. The last item is a chaise longue that's covered in a rich fuchsia-coloured fabric, maybe velvet. They put it in the centre of the lawn, facing the street. A car pulls up, an old maroon Mercedes with an English number plate. A man gets out and walks to the front door. He unlocks it, flinging it wide open. A woman gets out of the passenger door. She goes to the chaise longue and sits into the corner of it, wrapping the tails of her black coat around her legs. The coat has a sheen, like satin. She takes a book from her handbag and begins to read.

The man is sometimes on the driveway, sometimes in the house. He directs the removal men until the only item left is the pink sofa, the woman still tucked in its corner. He puts his hand on her shoulder and she follows him inside. A single bulb comes on in the living room. The woman stands at the window, looking out, while the furniture is dragged into place behind her.

Róisín's mother opens her eyes wide as if she's trying to stay awake. Her tiredness is showing in the dinner. Gammon steak, oven chips, sweetcorn from a tin. She passes Róisín a knife and fork. Her hand is the colour of the meat. After Róisín's dad left she got a job as a nurse's aid in the hospice. She used to play badminton and go to keep-fit classes. Now she washes people who are dying. How was school? she says. Her voice is cheery and tight.

Fine. The new people moved into Number 8.

I saw that.

They have a cool car.

The car is nice, but that old furniture is going to look odd in one of those bungalows.

I like it.

Did you get your homework done?

Some of it, she says. Her books are still on the table in the other room, unopened.

Her mother washes the dishes, working so fast the plates are still slick with grease. She tuts when Róisín drops them back in the basin.

Her mother goes into the front room. She switches on the television and lies on the couch. Róisín brings her books upstairs. The woman across the street is still at the window, as if she's been there all this time. She sees Róisín and holds her hand up. Róisín takes a step to the right and pulls down her blind.

The skip outside Number 8 is full. Róisín looks inside it. They've dumped things her mother is proud of. Rolls of patterned carpet, louvred doors, cork tiles. The front door opens.

Hello, the woman calls. Her hair is wet, and she has on blue suede cowboy boots and a brown corduroy pinafore. I'm Anna, she says.

Hiya. I'm Róisín.

Is that a Belfast accent?

Yeah.

Oh good. I'm not the only stranger in town.

You're English, says Róisín.

Afraid so. Oliver is Irish, though. He's a medical herbalist. We're going to use half the house as his clinic.

Maybe you'd be free at the weekend to give us a hand? We'll pay you, of course.

I'll ask my mum, says Róisín.

Her mother is bent over the fireplace. She pulls out the damper and smoke is sucked up the chimney.

I was talking to the woman across the road. Anna, her name is, says Róisín.

They're gutting the place.

She says they're putting a clinic in it.

I heard that.

He's a medical herbalist.

A cowboy, no doubt. She seems nice, but.

She asked me to help them at the weekend. She said she'd pay me.

Great! she says. It's the first time she's smiled in weeks. Róisín's dad doesn't give them enough money.

The deal floorboards have been sanded and stained a honey colour. Róisín has painted all the doors and skirting boards and window frames. She has become expert at it, applying the thick gloss with a vague criss-cross motion so as not to leave brush marks. They pay her at the end of every day, the notes counted out carefully. She'd do it for free but accepts the cash so they don't think she has nothing better to be doing.

Today they're going to unpack the tea chests. Anna prises open the one nearest the door. It's full to the lid of knick-knacks and ornaments wrapped in newspaper. Anna tells the story of each object as she takes it out. Róisín follows her around the house as she finds places for them. They prop a series of Victorian anatomical drawings on the long bookcase in Oliver's consulting room. Róisín peers at them. The writing is faint and tiny and in Latin and she can't figure out what organs they represent. They hang three flying ducks on the wall in the kitchen. Anna says they are supposed to look ironic but she's not sure. There is a pair of chunky vases in murky shades of brown and green that Anna puts at either end of the mantelpiece. She says they are mid-century. She makes it sound like a good thing, but they remind Róisín of her granny's house. There are three glass paper-weights with swirls of colour inside, shades from jade to turquoise to teal.

Where should we put these? says Anna.

Róisín lines them diagonally across the coffee table, smallest to largest.

Anna puts her arm around her waist. That's what I would have done, she says. Róisín looks down at the hand on her hip.

Anna says it's time for coffee. She brews it in a pot on the gas and boils milk for Róisín's. She lays out three small cups without handles. There is a bowl of dates on the kitchen table. Róisín doesn't like them but takes one so as not to seem unsophisticated. The coffee is bitter and she likes the heat of the cup in her hand. Anna knocks the kitchen window. Oliver is in the garden, hacking at the yew hedge with a saw. Anna says she likes yews. They remind her of old cemeteries. She'd like to put stone tablets in the ground carved with ghastly inscriptions.

The back door opens. Oliver steps out of his boots and crosses the floor in his socks. His feet are ugly. Broad and short, the toes all the same length, like a hobbit. He sits back in the chair as Anna bends around him. Pouring, placing the sugar bowl by his right hand, turning the cup so he's looking at it from the prettiest angle. She lays her hands on his shoulders and puts her mouth to his ear. She kisses him and says something in a voice Róisín can't hear. He is sitting very still. He lifts the cup and drinks it in one go.

There is a tall mahogany cabinet in the consulting room. The upper part has glass doors and shelves that they line with old medicine bottles. Their labels have beautiful names. Linden, valerian, opium, feverfew, belladonna. Anna says they are filled with coloured water. The base has a dozen drawers with crystal knobs. Most of Oliver's herbs will go in those. The dangerous ones will be locked away.

They are finished by three. Anna calls Oliver from the garden. He stands at the back door and takes his wallet from his pocket, his forehead crimping as he leafs slowly through the notes.

You don't need to pay me for today, says Róisín.

That's very kind, he says. He looks relieved. Anna walks her to the front door. Wait here, she says and goes into the living room. She comes back with a small picture in a frame. A blue-green mountain under a grey sky, the sun a tallowy smudge in the top right-hand corner. There's a book too, a thin cracked paperback with a woman in a garden on the front of it.

Róisín makes a cheese sandwich while the kettle is boiling. She makes a mug of coffee. Her mother buys instant granules; it tastes burnt and she can't drink it. She brings the book and the painting upstairs to her room. There's a clip frame above her headboard full of photos of her with the girls. She takes it down and puts it behind her chest of drawers. In its place she hangs the one Anna gave her and lies on her bed to read the book.

By the time her mother comes home, Róisín has lit the fire and finished all her homework. They eat crispy pancakes and coleslaw in front of the television.

Are you seeing any of the girls? her mother says.

No.

I hope you haven't fallen out with them.

No, she says. They have taken to imitating Róisín's accent when she speaks. *How. Now. Came. Name.* The teachers must hear them, everyone else can, but they don't do anything. The book Anna gave her is short, under a hundred pages. She finishes it before *The Late Late Show* is over.

Anna is patting primroses into a pot on her doorstep. She crosses the road as Róisín and her mother are getting into the car to go to Mass. She says Róisín has done trojan work.

I finished that book, says Róisín.

You've read a Russian novel, says Anna. How many girls in your class can say that?

It's not really a novel, more a long short story, says Róisín.

Well, it's Russian and it's a book.

Róisín's mother is smiling when she pulls out of the driveway.

The girls are at the back of the church with boys from the Christian Brothers school. When they see her their hands fly up to their mouths. She doesn't think about them when she's in Anna's house, but feels a lick of fear at the thought of school tomorrow. She hurries up the side aisle to a pew near the front. Her mother slides in beside her.

Not a bit like you to be so devout, she says.

Róisín reads two or three books a week now. She has gone up a grade in English, French and history. In her summer report her teachers commented on the improvement in her behaviour. It's hard to behave badly when you spend most of your time alone. The drips at the front are nice.

One of them writes poems about 'love and death and stuff'. She hasn't shown them to Róisín.

Oliver and Anna have gone out. Róisín is 'manning the phones'. The clinic has grown busy. A woman who writes for a Sunday newspaper went to Oliver for a cure for chronic psoriasis. In the article she said the 'handsome, faintly dishevelled witch doctor mixed her a tincture of turmeric, burdock and milk thistle that cleared her livid skin in days'. Cars pull up with number plates from all over the country. People from the town go to him too.

She gets the Hoover from the spare room, runs it around the waiting room, rearranges the magazines.

The phone rings. It's her mother.

What are you ringing me for?

I wondered where you were. She sounds sleepy.

You know where I am.

She drags the Hoover into Oliver's consulting room and leaves it in the middle of the floor. There's a heavy leather-bound book on his desk. The entry for belladonna is marked with a ribbon. It gives the history, the taxonomy, the side effects of poisoning. She tries the desk drawer. Notebooks, pens, pencils, scissors, a roll of freezer bags, small scales. There's a metal filing cabinet in the corner behind her. It holds the patients' records. She goes to the front door to check that it's locked. Back in the room she lifts the files out. She sits in Oliver's chair and begins to read.

The personal information is on the front page. Name, address, telephone number. Date of birth. Marital status. GP. The medical history is on the second page. Oliver writes a full-page report for each visit. Miss Liddy, her geography teacher, is being treated for sleep disturbance. At night she wakes panting, thinking she's had sex with a woman. Oliver has blended her a tea from liquorice, lemon balm, nettle and cleavers. Róisín smiles. In school they call her Liddy the Lezzer. Mrs Marren from three doors up is so depressed she can't get off the floor some days. He is treating her with St John's wort. There's a file for Tina. Róisín reads it twice and puts all the folders away, checking that they are in the correct order before closing the drawer.

The living room smells of turf and incense. There are black grapes in a crystal bowl on the coffee table. An old Scrabble set. The paperweights in a diagonal, where Róisín left them. Their bedroom is off it, behind double doors; the previous owners used it as a dining room. The malty smell of sleeping bodies. A pile of soft pastel clothes in the corner, Oliver's shoes lined up under the radiator. A half-drunk glass of water on a scuffed trunk that serves as a bedside table. A pop-up book beside it. Róisín thinks it's a children's book until she opens it up. A man and a woman are sitting on a four-poster bed. Both are naked, their private parts very close, legs pointing straight up in the air, soles of their feet touching like praying hands. She pulls the tag and the man's penis disappears into the woman's vagina. Róisín pulls the tag again, slowly at first, then faster. Their faces are serene, despite all the friction down below. On the next page the man and woman are straddling an elephant, still facing each other. Róisín pulls the tag and they rock back and forth. The doorbell rings. She puts the book back and runs from the room.

It's a Guard. He asks for Oliver.

They're out. I'm just answering the phone, she says. Her ears are hot.

And where are you from?

Belfast.

What are you doing here?

I live across the road. Do you want to leave a message? I'll get him again.

Róisín puts away the vacuum cleaner and sits on a chair in the waiting room. They come back an hour later. Anna looks around vaguely and goes straight to the bedroom. Oliver tells Róisín he'll pay her tomorrow. She is over the doorstep when she remembers the Guard. Oliver widens his eyes for a second. Right, he says.

Róisín rings three times but no one answers. Eventually Anna opens the front door. She hesitates, as if she's forgotten something. She starts to walk towards Oliver's consulting room, pauses and goes into the living room. Róisín follows her. She has been sitting in the dark. Róisín opens the curtains. She can see it then, the pillowy welt under her left eye.

What happened you? Róisín says.

I tripped. Snagged my cowboy boot on the leg of the coffee table and went flying. Her voice is dull.

The largest paperweight is split in two, the others just as they were. Róisín picks up one of the pieces. The colour at the centre was made by a knot of plastic.

That's the worst of it, Anna says. Finding out it's so much less than it looked. Just a crappy bit of tat cased in glass. Probably made in bloody Taiwan.

Oliver's car rolls up the driveway. Anna pulls Róisín on to the chaise longue. Tell me what you've been reading, she says. She used to choose books for Róisín. She helps herself now, making her way along the bookcase in the living room, shelf by shelf, when she's finished cleaning.

I'm reading *The White Album*. Joan Didion's just been sent to buy clothes for Linda Kasabian to wear to the Manson trial.

Anna is distracted, her eyes going from Róisín to the door. She keeps licking her lips. Oliver comes in, dressed in the green tweed suit he wears when he goes out. His glasses are near the tip of his nose.

Anna tries to stand up. She misjudges her footing and sinks back down. Maybe you could come back another time, Róisín, Oliver says. He doesn't look at her.

Róisín goes to the noticeboard in the hall to see what class she's been put in. Different room, same girls. She chooses a seat in the centre of the front row. There are giggles as she takes her books out. Tina says something in a northern accent. She's sitting on her desk, legs swinging, face lit with malice.

Don't mind her, says the girl who writes poetry, as she slides into the chair beside her. Róisín smiles.

At breaktime Róisín stays in the classroom. She waits until Tina gets up to leave and follows her to the toilets. Tina has her hand on the furthest door. Róisín shoves her into the cubicle.

Are you going in to change your nappy?

What?

I said are you going in to change your nappy.

I don't know what you're talking about.

You do. And unless you want everyone else in the school talking about it, you'll keep out of my way. You horrible cunt.

Tina comes back to class just as the bell rings. Her face is red. She glances at Róisín. The look is full of fear.

Róisín's mother is in the hallway. Why are you up, Mum? she says.

I couldn't sleep with that carry-on across the road.

Róisín goes to the window. Oliver's car is gone and the curtains are still drawn. What carry-on?

Anna came out on to the street in her nightdress at about half eleven. She had lipstick all over her face.

Where was Oliver?

He was with a patient. He wasn't long coming out, with the guldering out of her.

Where are they now?

She's in hospital.

Is she sick?

That's putting it mildly. Men-in-white-coats job, a couple of Guards.

Róisín sits at the table in the front room and takes her books out. She begins doing sums, loses her place, opens and closes her history book. Her mother brings her a plate of spaghetti and kisses her hair. Anna'll be all right, she says and leaves for work.

Róisín goes upstairs after ten. The driveway of Number 8 is still empty. She lies on her bed. Every time she hears a car engine she goes to the window, but Oliver doesn't come back. How different it was in the beginning, the lightness in Anna. The day they spent opening boxes, afternoons talking about books. It was funny, the way she was with Oliver. Fussing over him, her fingers reaching for his sleeve, his hand. The way he sat so still, watching her, saying so little.

Róisín is eating a bowl of cereal when her mother comes in from work. She sits at the kitchen table and lights a cigarette.

Did somebody die? says Róisín. Her mother only smokes when she's had a bad night.

A child, she says. Her eyes are bloodshot.

I made my own sandwich.

Good girl.

Last year Róisín arrived at school almost late every day, to avoid the jeering and muttering. Today she is early. Tina's head is down as she passes. They sit through a double class of Irish. The back row is silent.

At breaktime, a couple of the girls hover by Róisín's desk. You work for that herbalist, one says.

I do, says Róisín. She bends back over her book. They move away.

By lunchtime they can bear it no more. One says she heard Anna wrote crazy words in lipstick on her arms and legs. Another says she was naked. Someone else says that Oliver is on the run. Róisín thinks of the last time she was in their house, his tone of voice when he told her to come back another time, without so much as a glance at her. She crushes the foil she wrapped her sandwich in. Tina is lurking at the side, watching Róisín through her fringe. Róisín had forgotten how good it feels to have eyes on her, waiting for her to speak.

He's weird, she says. I think he was beating her.

She tells them about the shattered paperweight, how carefully Anna moved around Oliver. The astrakhan coat he gave her, made from the fleeces of aborted lambs. The dirty book he keeps in plain sight, a pop-up Kama Sutra, the fucking pervert. The dangerous herbs that are locked away, she never found out where. Anna's symptoms, she says, are consistent with belladonna poisoning. Hallucinations. Dry mouth. Agitation. Tiredness.

Oliver's car is on the driveway. Róisín's mother comes down the stairs.

He's back, says Róisín.

He is, God help him.

God help him nothing.

Anna has problems. Oliver met her when he was doing voluntary work. She used to take a lot of drugs.

A Guard came to the door looking for him. What was that about?

He was supposed to register his car within 180 days of arriving in Ireland. The Guard was just reminding him.

Róisín runs upstairs and bolts herself into the bathroom, the only room in the house with a lock. She doesn't need to see her mother to know she's at the bottom of the stairs, frowning, with half her bottom lip between her teeth.

A red hatchback mounts the kerb. It's the first car Róisín has seen at the house for months. Oliver comes down the path. Behind him, the house looks vacant. An old couple get out of the car. He puts his arms round the woman. He takes the man's hands in his and holds them for a long time. They wait on the kerb as Oliver fills the boot. Two big green suitcases, a tartan holdall, a couple of cardboard boxes. The blue cowboy boots, the astrakhan coat on a hanger. He smooths the fur with his hands and pulls the door down. It's then that Róisín sees Anna in the back seat. She's strapped in like a child, an anorak zipped up to her chin. She closes her eyes and lies back against the headrest as they pull away. Oliver watches until the car leaves the cul de sac. He starts up the path and pauses to right the FOR SALE sign again. This time the shaft has been broken. It is still swaying as he closes the door of Number 8.

IMBOLC

Elaine hauled Grace out of her cot and slung her on to her hip. The other baby, the one in her belly, she was carrying low, and there wasn't much room. She went along the hall. Liam had put turf in the range before he left for the lambing shed and the kitchen was warm and quiet. She squashed Grace into her highchair and put on a pan of milk for their breakfast.

She stood at the sink and looked up at the hill farm. They still called it that, even though Liam's father had lost the rest of the farm, the good land further down the mountain, where he'd once kept a dairy herd. They just had sheep now. A few of them were dotted around the fields, their coats grubby against the snow. It had begun to fall late the previous evening, and Liam had been out for most of the night, bringing in the ewes. The ruined byre where they stored the turf was now a rounded knoll and the hedges and stone walls were fringed white. Only the lambing shed was bare, snowflakes melting on contact with the roof, trickling down the green corrugated ridges. Around the edge of the structure was a grey-brown slush.

She heard the engine before she saw the car, if you'd call it a car. A 4x4, high off the ground and glossy black, its rear portion long, with tinted windows; a hearse on steroids. It crunched to a halt in the yard, leaving thick bluish tracks in its wake. Liam came out of the shed, wiping his hands on his arse. He stood back and watched the brother and sister get out. Trevor Rainey, his humped shoulders putting ten years on him, his nose and mouth wrapped in a scarf to keep the weather from his bad lungs. Stacey Rainey, in leopard-print wellingtons, twisting her auburn hair into a messy bun. When Liam had said he was taking Trevor's sister on as an Agricultural Science placement student, Elaine had thought he meant the other girl, the one with stumpy legs and a squint. They followed Liam into the shed.

Elaine put four Weetabix into a pasta bowl and doused it in hot milk. She sat at the table to share it with Grace. One for you, one for me, she told the child, but Grace was hungry and after a couple of mouthfuls Elaine amended it to two for you, one for me. Grace hadn't swallowed the last spoonful when she seized the tray of the high-chair with both hands. Evacuating her bowels, her face a picture of both horror and bliss. Elaine dropped the bowl and spoon in the sink and brought Grace to the bedroom.

She lay her on the bed to change her. There seemed to be more shite than child. She wrapped the soiled nappy tightly, resealing the adhesive strips, and pitched it across the room at the bin. It landed safely. Yes, she said and punched the air. Grace clapped. Elaine sat Grace in the shower tray where she slapped at shampoo suds. A bath would have eased Elaine's backache but lately it appalled her to see the new baby heave from one side to another, to feel the tiny heels and hands jab between her ribs.

Elaine dried Grace first, taking care with the folds at her knees and thighs and neck, and blew a raspberry on her tummy. She dressed her and put her into the cot while she got herself ready. A couple of months earlier, the bath sheet had wrapped all the way around her. Now her bare belly ballooned from it. She was colossal. In the sallow gloom of the energy-saver bulb her nipples were like cigar butts. New stretch marks made a violet lacy pattern on either side of her diaphragm. The line that ran from her bulging navel to the unkempt pubic hair that she rarely saw made her look as though she had been marked for dissection. She snapped the straps of her bra up to her collarbone and rubbed wheatgerm oil into her itchy skin. She pulled on maternity leggings, one of Liam's shirts, and Gryffindor striped knee socks bought long before a shopping trip meant standing in the baby clothes section of Penneys trying to remember what she had gone in for. There was more hair on her hairbrush than in her fringe and she spat coral-coloured froth when she brushed her teeth. A midwife at the clinic had told her she should have given herself more time before planning another baby. There had been no plan. Just enough Pinot Grigio to help her overlook the resemblance that Liam's cock bore to Grace's arm.

In the kitchen, she put Grace in her playpen and resumed her watch at the window. Snow was still falling. The shed door opened and Liam came out with Trevor Rainey. They gripped hands as if they were about to arm-wrestle, a gangsta gesture that filled her with shame for her husband. For herself.

She made tea and sat at the table to drink it. If the weather hadn't turned, she would have driven towards town. Picked up biscuits and crisps for them to snack on in the shed. Called in on Siobhán, her sister, although Elaine found the lodge depressing, with its smell of hash and mildew, the mad talk out of Sid, as if he was living on the edge of a vast frontier. For want of something better to do she stripped the bed and bunged the linen in the machine to wash.

At eleven, she dressed Grace in her pink pram suit and put on one of Liam's coats, stepping into her wellingtons at the back door. She went up the lane slowly, her boots leaving deep, deliberate prints. Grace had tilted her head back and was flicking her tongue out, catching snowflakes.

The shed was warm, the air fetid with damp wool and blood and sheep droppings. There were ewes crammed into the big pen, pawing and fretting, heavy bellies skimming the floor. In the small pens, the new mothers were nuzzling and lapping at their newborns. Stacey Rainey was filling a bucket of water at the sink by the wall, dressed in a Letterkenny IT Gaelic football jersey that was a size too small and black wet-look jeggings. She put the bucket in one of the pens and came to Elaine. She tickled Grace under the chin and the child's mouth gaped open, a slobbery, happy smile. The wee traitor, thought Elaine. Where's Liam? she said.

Stacey inclined her head at the far wall. He's watering. We're afraid the pipes'll freeze.

We're afraid – the cheek of her.

When are you back to college? said Elaine.

Monday week.

Great, said Elaine.

A panel in the false wall slid aside. For a moment Elaine glimpsed the rows and rows of plants, the cables and lamps that were strung across the ceiling, their eerie light. Liam banged the panel shut and crossed the floor to her, his feet kicking up the lime-slaked straw.

Stay in the house, I told you, he said.

I'm bored.

I don't want Grace breathing in this shit. He kissed his daughter on the forehead.

What time will you be down for lunch? said Elaine.

Half twelve.

She put Grace on her other hip. As she passed the big pen, a ewe moaned, a dreadful sound. She called out to Liam to tell him the animal seemed ready, but his back was to her. He was standing with his legs wide apart, talking down to Stacey Rainey, who was crouching on the floor, bottle-feeding a lamb through the bars of one of the pens. Her haunches in the leggings were full and shiny. That one's a tramp, she whispered to Grace as they went through the door to the yard. The clouds were low and pinkish. The gritter hadn't made it and beyond the lower fields the road was a lethal grey ribbon.

Elaine left her boots at the back door, caked now with snow and wet straw. She made more tea, a bottle for Grace. She put her in the highchair but couldn't settle herself at the table. Stacey Rainey was knickerless and wearing false eyelashes. In a lambing shed. Elaine went back to the window and ate two KitKats.

Liam came down the hill alone. He soaped his arms to the shoulders at the sink in the utility room before entering the kitchen. Well, he said. He lifted Grace from the highchair and rubbed his nose against hers. She laughed and patted his cheeks.

Elaine slid a SuperValu lasagne in front of him. It had little meat and a crimson sauce. He ate with Grace on his knee, his arm draped easily around her.

Is herself not having any lunch? said Elaine.

She said she'd wait till after I have mine.

That's good of her.

It was supposed to sound sarcastic, but Liam said, It was.

Sorry about the lasagne. I couldn't get out to the shop.

It's grand.

It looks shite.

It's shite enough, all right.

Jesus. I said I was sorry.

You said it was shite first.

I said I'm sorry.

Fuck's sake, he said and pushed the empty tray away. Are you all right today?

I don't like you getting mixed up with that shower.

What planet are you on, Elaine? I need help, and in case you haven't noticed, I'm kind of restricted in who I can let into that shed. He handed Grace to her and left, slamming the back door behind him.

Elaine put the lasagne tray in the bin and filled the kettle. Liam had paused at the top of the lane and was looking up at the clean roof. He crossed the yard. At the shed door, he tilted his face to the sky, as if he was asking for strength, before pulling it open. He held it wide until Stacey came out in a cropped jacket that made her legs look even longer. They stood facing each other for a few seconds, the girl putting her hands behind her head as if he'd pulled a gun on her, then liberating her hair. She turned from him slowly and began to walk away. Liam's chin went up, as if he was calling out to her, and she swung round, walking backwards as she replied to him. His shoulders heaved the way they did when he thought something was funny. He went through the door, closing it behind him. At the edge of the yard Stacey Rainey stopped and looked back at the shed. She pushed her hands into her pockets and traipsed down the lane, the leopard-print boots fitting neatly in the footprints Elaine had made.

She knocked at the back door and came in shyly. Hiya, she said from the utility room. Elaine stood by the table, holding Grace, and watched the girl wash her unseasonably bronzed arms, the glister of soap and water on them.

I haven't much in, said Elaine, but I can make you a sandwich.

Stacey took a protein bar from her pocket and waved it vaguely. I have this, she said, but I'd love a cup of tea.

The kettle clicked off and Elaine put Grace in the highchair and gave her a rusk.

When are you due? Stacey asked Elaine's belly.

Six weeks, she said, dropping a teabag in a mug and dunking it up and down with a spoon.

Irish twins, they call it, when you have two babies in the one year.

Elaine felt her face get hot. We wanted to have them close together, she said, putting the mug on the table and sitting beside Grace.

Stacey took a bite of her bar and chewed for a long time. The boys are worried, she said.

About the water freezing?

No. About the roof. That's how they're catching people now. The clean roof is a dead giveaway. A sign of heat.

Yeah, I know, said Elaine. Only she didn't know. One crop, Liam had told her, to clear their debts. He'd grow it and Trevor Rainey would sell it. He'd said it as though Trevor was his business partner and not his main creditor. Elaine hadn't protested. Do what you have to do, she'd said. I don't want to know.

They're going to wait and see how long the snow goes on for. The lambing is a good cover, but the sheep don't generate that much heat by themselves, said Stacey.

Elaine was filled with pity for her. She was eighteen, twenty at most. For all her glamour, it was naive the way she spoke, repeating things she'd overheard the men say, trying to sound worldly. And what sort of brother was Trevor Rainey, sending his teenage sister to shovel shite in a grow house?

How many ewes are left to go? said Elaine.

Thirty-odd. Liam says we'll be done by the weekend.

Not so bad. You'll be glad when it finishes.

Ah no. The wee lambs are cute, said Stacey. Anyways, I'd better go back up and do a bit. Thanks for the tea.

Grace was still hungry. Elaine reheated some of the stew she'd made the previous day, flaking the meat with a fork and squashing it into the gravy and soggy carrots. She put the plastic bowl in front of Grace and watched her gather food in her fists and push it into her mouth. You mucky wee article, she said softly. She poured herself a glass of milk and sat at the table, but her gut was sick with worry and she couldn't even lift it to her lips; all this was her fault.

The men from the Sheriff's Office had come the week Elaine did the pregnancy test. Liam had been bulling, roaming the place in quiet fury, hardly talking to her. On the fourth day she rose early and dressed in normal clothes, not the glorified pyjamas she'd been wearing for months. She applied make-up and took tongs to her hair, trying to look the way she used to, before she'd become sluggish and throughother. She cooked him a fry-up, chattering away as he ate. When the food was gone he tossed his cutlery on to the plate, as if he was throwing down a gauntlet. You gave me the green light, he said, in a voice so steady it frightened her. It was as if by letting him part her legs she had given a signal that he could work away at her without consequence.

Then they'd heard the engines, a car followed by a truck. Elaine went to the front door, the entrance they never used. She opened it to three of them, a slight man in a grey suit flanked by two shaven-headed men in bulky black jackets like bouncers wear. She caught the pair exchanging a look, amused, she suspected, at being greeted by a plump dolly bird with a baby over her shoulder. The suit asked for Liam and held out a plastic card, his ID.

That'd be me, said Liam, from behind her. He stepped off the porch and stood in front of the older man. You're the one with the badge, he said. I suppose this pair have the gun and the horse.

The men seemed to fill the house. One of them lifted the flatscreen TV off the wall in the living room. He'd put on gloves and looked for all the world like a burglar. The other asked her if they had any games consoles or laptops. The suit was trailing them from room to room, writing in a notebook.

Liam was sitting at the kitchen table in front of the dirty plate, a thumb pressed into the apple of his cheek, fingers splayed at his hairline. How much do they want? Elaine hissed at him.

Nine grand.

Ring someone.

Who can I ring?

I don't care, she'd said. Just get them out of this house.

Grace had finished her lunch. Elaine set about her with a series of wipes and carried her to the bedroom to change her nappy. The bed was unmade, but they got into it anyway, Elaine laying Grace on the mattress protector, which had yellowed on Liam's side. His pillow seemed to bear an imprint of his face, like the Shroud of Turin. Grace fell asleep in seconds, fingers on Elaine's cheeks. Her face creased suddenly, as if she was having a row with someone, and just as quick slumped into a drunk-looking smile. The other baby was still, and Elaine felt herself sink into the place between waking and sleeping. She dreamt, a vivid waking dream from which she couldn't rouse herself. Two Guards were in the doorway of the shed. The panel on the false wall was open and the grow house looked like a strange film that was playing on a vast screen. Liam was pulling his hand from inside a ewe. Stacey Rainey was behind him, pointing her tits at his back. A car horn woke her. She jolted, frightening Grace from her nap.

A mist was curling around her father's battered Corolla. There was a mantle of snow on the roof and a new scratch by the keyhole on the driver's door, deep this time. She could picture him outside the Mountain Inn in the dark, a lit Carroll's in the corner of his mouth, trying to find the lock. He leaned to kiss Grace, a yeasty hum from his breath. Elaine was annoyed, yet relieved that she could only smell beer. It meant he had been in the pub drinking with other people, not alone in a torpor of whiskey and grief.

You're happier to see me than your mother is, he said to Grace, reaching out his arms to her. Elaine swung the child away from him.

Are you all right to take her?

Can I not come up here without you giving me a hard time?

Elaine relented, handed Grace over. I'm worried about you. You can't be driving round the place langers. You'll kill yourself or someone else. Or get banned.

He sat on a chair at the table and jiggled Grace up and down on his knees. He opened his legs, let her slip almost to the floor. She looked terrified then dissolved into giggles as he pulled her back up.

You're a dose, he said. I only go out for the few pints and the company.

That road must be like a skating rink.

I took it handy.

Had you anything to eat? I might put on a few rashers for a sandwich. He came and stood beside her at the sink. The shed door opened and Stacey Rainey came into the yard and took out her phone.

He elbowed Elaine gently. I'd be laying off the rasher sandwiches if I were you, he said, and himself inside in the shed with that one.

Jesus, Daddy, said Elaine. She went to the utility room and emptied the tumble drier, bringing the clothes to the table.

Her father put Grace in her playpen and began folding. He made a stack of Grace's things then one of white clothes, 'newborn' vests and Babygros that Elaine had laundered ready for her hospital bag. She watched him pair tiny socks and was moved terribly by the deftness of his thick fingers, the roughness of his hands against the delicate fabric.

Are you crying? he said.

No. I'm just tired. Liam's up there morning, noon and night and I'm not sleeping.

Go on up to him. I'll mind Grace.

Outside the light was fading. She brought her phone in case she needed to use the torch. There was a message from Siobhán. *Happy St Brigid's Day, you goddess.* *Nutter*, Elaine replied, followed by three love hearts. The footprints she'd left earlier had almost disappeared and the fields had deepened to a cold blue-white. She paused in the doorway of the shed, fearful of gleaning an ease, an intimacy between her husband and the young student. She needn't have worried. Liam was tending to the torn backside of one of the ewes. Stacey Rainey was as far away from the animal as possible, looking as if she was about to vomit. Liam asked her for more catgut and glared at her as she dithered. Eventually she handed him a piece that was too short.

It's not for flossing my fucking teeth, he said.

Elaine put down her phone and took the roll of catgut from Stacey, noticing the girl's bitten nails and the fake tan that had collected in the webbing between her fingers and thumbs. She cut a length and threaded the needle. She passed it to Liam and handed him scissors as he finished stitching.

Fill up those buckets again, he told Stacey, without looking up. He held out his arms and Elaine wiped the red, sticky mess from them. That wee fella needs a couple of nights by the range, he said, pointing at a skinny, foetal-looking creature that was squirming in a plastic crate lined with newspaper.

I'll take him with me now, she said. He wrapped the animal in an old towel and put it in her arms.

She held the lamb inside her coat. Halfway down the hill she felt in her pockets. She had left her phone behind. She turned and went back to the shed. Her eyes took a moment to adjust to the light, and at first she didn't know what she was seeing. Stacey was bent over the sink, clutching its sides. Liam was behind her, one hand on the wall, the other holding her hair. Stacey's orange buttocks were bouncing as if he was riding a pony. Liam turned towards the doorway, where Elaine was standing. He held her gaze, a look of hatred on his face.

Elaine took her phone and went outside. Phone Trevor Rainey, she'd begged Liam as the men were moving around their house, even though she knew he only had cash because he was dodgy. When the black jeep pulled up half an hour later and the television was back on the wall, she'd felt relief. Afterwards she had opened a beer and served it to Liam at the kitchen table. We'll pay him back, she told him, her fingers in his hair, it'll be grand. He flung her hand off him and it dropped heavily by her side. Are you that fucking stupid? he said.

The blue of the fields seemed to drain the air of light, and with all that she was carrying, she couldn't see her feet. She tried to turn on the torch but couldn't manage it. Her feet sank deep in the snow and each step was exhausting. A sob was bulging at the back of her throat. She swallowed it down. Her father was at the sink, holding Grace. He lifted the child's hand in a wave. Elaine raised hers in reply and trudged towards them, the lamb trembling in her arms.

BEYOND CARTHAGE

It had begun at dawn as they got off the plane, sparse plashes on the runway. By the time the coach deposited them at the Marhaba Aparthotel it was a slanted, dancing deluge. For three days they had been lying on their narrow beds, eating crisps and reading the guidebooks they should have read before the holiday was booked. From time to time they went to the balcony to examine the sky for a break in the clouds. Therese did not feel entitled to complain. Noreen had wanted to go to the Canary Islands, which according to Sky News were enjoying lows of twenty-one degrees Celsius. The same forecast assured them that the band of low pressure hanging over the northern tip of Africa would move off late on Tuesday. Their last night.

Therese had wanted to go somewhere exotic. To wander through a bazaar crammed with pyramids of heady spices, to drink amber-hued mint tea from a gold-painted glass. She had wanted to eat rich meats with her fingers while belly dancers and snake charmers whirled around her. She had wanted to go to Morocco or Egypt, but in her haste to get away had got mixed up. They were in Tunisia, not in a Berber village or by a Phoenician ruin, but in a purpose-built concrete resort arranged around a new marina, as neat and airless as an architect's model. Government-controlled souvenir shops and blocky, modern cafes lined a promenade edged with palm trees still so tender they coiled in on themselves in the gales. To be fair, the Mediterranean was just a few yards away. They had seen it once, when a wave broke across the sea wall and sent turbid water frothing over their shoes.

The waiter brought their cappuccinos. Noreen took out her phone and began scrolling through her messages. Therese left hers in her bag, so she wouldn't be tempted to check again if Donal had replied. She recognised the couple beside them from the flight. They were sitting in silence, their chairs turned to face the sea, shuffling coins around on their table. They flagged down the waiter and paid him. As he counted the money, the woman said, Every time you turn there's one with a hand out. Young local men sat in clusters, smoking cigarettes and drinking shots of coffee. Some were with Dutch or German women who spoke English with heavy accents and traced smiley faces in the condensation on their beer glasses. There was clearly a want in them. What were they like, flirting with nineteen-year-olds they were old enough to have reared? And what could a boy like that see in a menopausal woman with bad highlights and a parched cleavage?

Noreen put her phone down and took a sip of her coffee. Jesus, she said.

What's wrong?

Mammy's giving out about the Meals on Wheels. Says she won't see a proper dinner till I'm back. The bowels will be *trína chéile* for the next fortnight. How are your lot?

Grand, said Therese. A stream of messages had come from Donal the previous evening. *Enjoy, you deserve it. We miss you so much.* He'd sent a video of a labradoodle playing the Moonlight Sonata on a baby grand, which was most unlike him. He'd even used emojis. Maybe he really was sorry. Therese sent him a curt enquiry about the school run to which he still hadn't replied. She kept her emojis to herself.

We need to find something to do later, said Noreen.

Will we have a look through the brochures?

I've looked already. All those places are outside, she said. It's bucketing. And I'm choosing today. If there's nothing else shaking I'm going on the piss.

The previous day, Therese had suggested they go to the market in the next town. They took a taxi to the medina and wandered through a network of gloomy alleyways. They passed crates of small round turnips and radishes the size of tennis balls, bunches of mint and dill and savoury. Butchers were selling merguez and chunks of sinewy goat from kiosks that didn't have refrigeration. They saw no ceramics or leather goods or carpets, just tables laden with enamel saucepans and plastic utensils. When they emerged half an hour later, empty-handed, their taxi driver was still there.

He'd better not charge us for waiting, said Noreen.

The man let out a sigh and started the meter. The resort is very new, very nice. Why do you go to old dirty places?

We want to go where the locals go, said Therese.

Local people do not have a choice.

Well? Noreen was saying. Do I get to choose or what?

Yeah, said Therese. You can choose.

They paid the bill and zipped themselves back into their damp fleeces. On the way out of the cafe, Noreen picked up a flier and pushed it into her bag. They bent into the rain and ran back to the hotel.

In the room, they draped their wet things over a radiator. Noreen sat on her bed and took out the flier. She read it front and back and handed it to Therese.

This might be nice, she said. On one side there was a photograph of a young woman draped from neck to knee in the whitest towel, slim legs slanted stiffly to one side, skin glistening. Her kohled eyes were looking up at the camera. She was in a steamy room decorated with tiles in shades of turquoise and azure and gold. The price list for the Milk and Honey Hammam was on the other side. It's not cheap, but there's nothing to spend money on here, said Noreen. All I've bought is duty-free.

It's not the money. We should go on a trip. Maybe over towards Tunis.

I, said Noreen, wouldn't be into that.

Can you not go by yourself?

I don't want to go by myself! And you said I could choose.

Therese had booked the wrong resort in the wrong country in the wrong season. Oh, for God's sake, she said. I'll go if you come on a trip with me in the morning.

You're on. She went down to the desk to book the *total luxe package*.

Therese took out her phone. Nothing. She didn't want to talk to Donal, yet was annoyed by his silence. What was he at? Sending her cute videos and blushing emojis, then ignoring her.

Noreen came back and clapped her hands. They would be collected from the lobby at a quarter to three. She got two glasses from the bathroom and shook a bottle of rum at Therese, who prepared to explain again that drinking was a bad combination with the meds, that alcohol was a strong indicator for her strain of cancer. But she was tired of explaining, of denying herself. Feck it, she said. It's not much fun being good all the time.

Noreen let out a whoop that was too big for the room. She poured two drinks, putting so little Coke in her own it looked like ginger ale. She shook salted almonds into a bowl and they brought their glasses out to the covered balcony. The storm billowed across the street below. Taxis, their lights blurred, deposited and collected holidaymakers, pulling off slowly and turning left in the direction of the promenade. Therese looked at Noreen. Grim, she said.

It's not too bad.

You're just being nice.

It's great to get away.

Up to a point.

Noreen took their glasses inside to refill them. Maybe it wasn't so bad. Better than looking at Donal for the week.

If we're going to Tunis we might as well go the whole way. Beyond Carthage, said Therese.

I don't even know where I am now. I thought we were going to Lanzarote.

It was an ancient city. The ruins are well preserved, and they're a few miles after Tunis. Beyond them there's a lovely village.

Therese got the guidebook and showed her a double-page photograph. Whitewashed houses were built into a hillside so steep they seemed to overhang each other. Doors and windows and ironwork had been painted in shades of blue, and carpets of bougainvillea crept over walls and terraces. Blonde tourists sat on sun-bleached patios and looked out over the shimmering Bay of Tunis. Sidi Bou Said, she said.

It's hard to believe it's the same country, said Noreen.

A sudden gust caught some rain and threw it across the balcony. They went indoors.

Reception called to say their car had arrived. They weren't ready. Therese didn't have time to brush her teeth and her mouth was waxy from eating nuts. On the way down, Noreen answered everything Therese said with a loose laugh. When the lift doors opened, the few people who were sitting around the foyer were looking in their direction, Noreen's guffaws clearly audible from a couple of floors away. A tall, slim man in jeans and a suit jacket was waiting by the desk. He said his name was Giuseppe. He brought them outside to his car, a model of Fiat Therese had never seen before. Noreen sat in the front beside him.

Loving the motor, she said.

Giuseppe put a plastic card in a slot and the dashboard lit up.

Buongiorno, said a deep electronic male voice.

Buongiorno yourself, said Noreen and slapped her thigh. Her movements had become expansive and inaccurate, and she knocked her elbow against the back of Giuseppe's hand. The gold Rolex watch on his wrist was loose and made a tinny jangle.

Are you French, Giuseppe?

Italiano.

Very nice, said Noreen. Therese bit the inside of her cheeks to keep a laugh in. Noreen looked at her in the rear-view mirror and stuck her tongue out.

Giuseppe braked hard when he needed to slow and took corners in third gear. When they got out, Therese put her hands on the roof of the car to steady herself. The flier had shown a traditional bathhouse; they were outside the annexe to an office block, a flat-roofed concrete building with a row of high windows. Inside, they were greeted by a young woman wearing a white tunic and trousers, like a nurse's uniform. She was heavily made up, her hair covered by a scarf. She led them into a changing room, gave them baskets for their belongings. She handed each of them a towel and a piece of turquoise tissue paper. Noreen unfolded hers. It was a pair of disposable knickers. She held them up in front of Therese's face and tugged the elastic on the waistband in and out.

Ah here, said Therese.

They undressed with care, folding each garment as it was removed, placing it in the basket. The paper rustled beneath their towels as they wriggled into the surgical pants. Just as they were ready, Giuseppe came into the room. Therese looked around the walls and ceiling; he had come in so promptly she wondered had he been watching them on a monitor. She and Noreen stood side by side, their feet in white cotton slippers. Giuseppe stepped forward and tugged their towels away. It reminded Therese of a trick she had seen on TV when she was a child, involving a tablecloth and stacks of clattery china. Giuseppe looked at Therese's body for a second longer than was polite. His removal of the towel was so flamboyant he would lose face by giving it back to her. Noreen crossed her arms over her breasts. They squashed out above and below, blue-veined and creamy like Stilton.

He brought them into a steam-filled room with wooden benches around the walls. Rain dashed the windows. Condensation ran down beige tiles. It was like the changing rooms in the public pool at home.

Relax, said Giuseppe, an instruction that filled Therese with anxiety. He left the room.

At first they sat facing each other, Noreen giving the floor a stellar smile. At least you're thin, she said, without looking up. Then she stood. I'll come over beside you, she said.

Therese's moisturiser was trickling down her face and into her mouth. She could taste chemicals and salt. Noreen's face was deeply flushed, her eyes pink-streaked. It's a bit mad, she said.

Just a bit.

Probably normal for here, though.

Therese didn't think it was normal at all. Most of the local women covered their hair, wore long sleeves with loose trousers or ankle-length skirts. She doubted many of them came to the Milk and Honey to be stripped nearly naked by Giuseppe. Noreen leaned back and closed her eyes, lids flickering like a child feigning sleep. Therese looked down at herself. Her right aureole was beginning to dimple, the nipple hardening. Sweat was coursing steadily now, over her throat, down along her sternum, collecting under her breasts. After months spent trying to keep them dry, they felt slimy and dank.

Giuseppe came back with fresh towels. Therese wound hers around herself. Noreen pushed her chin forward and puffed out a jet of rummy breath. She draped her towel over her arm and winked at Therese as they followed him into the next room. He took their towels again and ushered them under the shower heads that ran along one wall. The tepid water was bracing after the hot steam. A man came in, shorter and older than Giuseppe. He was barefoot and holding a tin bucket. He went at whatever was in it with a brush, eyes lowered. Giuseppe said something to him in Arabic. The man knelt beside Noreen. He flicked a clot of mud at her thigh and spread it outwards, up and down, back and forth, until her haunch was covered.

Therese had an urge to flee but could only watch and wait. The man finished with Noreen and began to work on her. The mud was cold at first, then tight, the skin on her thighs and hips constricting as it dried. Her arms then, the brush skimming along the length of them and back. He twirled two fingers and she turned to face the wall. Long strokes now, the cloy of wet earth at the nape of her neck, in the elastic of the ludicrous turquoise knickers. Therese didn't feel drunk any more, just full of dread. She wanted to take the brush, smear herself in mud, cover her scars. Another twirl of his fingers and she could bear it no more.

No, she said. Thank you.

At first, when the tubes and drains had been removed, after the ragged blackened whorls had been shaved away, Therese had thought it looked pretty good. Clothed, her breasts looked better than ever; the left one had always been slightly bigger than the right and now they were the same size. She had refused a silicon implant. Even tooth whitening seemed unnatural to her, and she couldn't bear the idea of a pouch of chemicals under her skin. The flesh to make a new breast had been taken from her abdomen, leaving a flat stomach and a pink groove that smiled from hip to hip. The reconstruction was a patchwork of flesh in different shades and textures, some run through with silvery stretch marks, some tanned, all tacked on to the milky shreds of what the surgeons left behind.

Noreen's mud had dried to the dun-grey of a wallow-ing mammal. It cracked when she bent an arm to scratch herself. The man ran the shower and hunched under the water with her, scrubbing at her with a loofah, limb by limb, torso back then front, brown droplets flaying his white clothes. When he was done, Noreen stood freshly pink and smiling.

It was Therese's turn. Her scars grew bleary in the steam and splashing mud. Since the surgery she had thought about her skin differently, as though it was a fine veneer that mustn't be scraped or tarnished. Now it felt raw, new. The man's work was done. He bowed and backed away.

In the next room, an attempt had been made to temper the spartan buffness with candles and a diffuser that was panting sandalwood. Oud music was playing low in the background. Noreen claimed a massage table.

That sounds like *sean-nós*, she said. It's shite.

Therese lay down. In private, she could face her body, her scars. Exposed like this she had to take on the reactions of other people, had to absorb their discomfort, their revulsion. She had only managed to attend counselling twice, as the weekly trip to Dublin wasn't feasible. There was a support group in town, but she couldn't bear the thought of sharing her feelings with friends of friends, women she knew to see. The breast nurse in the hospital had given her a booklet that she read until she had learned it by heart, ticking off the phases as they passed. Her cancer became old news. She hadn't needed further treatment. She was still here.

Noreen shifted on to her side.

Are you all right, hun?

Fabulous.

Giuseppe came back in his shirtsleeves. He took off his cufflinks; they were showy like his watch. Therese wondered at a boy his age in such a get-up, the impression he was crafting. He raised his arm and poured oil from a height as if he was partaking in a sacrament. Therese looked at the ceiling. She tried not to think about the slaps his hands made as he pummelled at the mounds and troughs of Noreen Foley's body. She tried not to look but turned her head in time to see him clamp his palms over Noreen's breasts and move them in a circular motion, more erotic than therapeutic.

It was a glorified knocking shop, with a clientele of desperate women. Giuseppe dressed as he did to appeal to golf widows from northern Europe, to women who found themselves single at an age when being alone made them feel ridiculous. He probably wasn't even Italian. She and Noreen fitted right in.

Therese lay on her front with her face in the hole, her real breast flattened out and tingling at the graze of the towel, the new one a sturdy knot of flesh that felt nothing. He began at her tailbone and kneaded his way up to her shoulders. He hesitated then rolled her on to her back. The corner of her mouth was twitching.

Donal couldn't stand to touch it. Once she had taken his finger and pressed it to the skin between the seams. He had forced a smile but pulled away when she placed it where the nipple used to be. Afterwards he treated her to the full gamut of his foreplay repertoire, including a foray down below, which she didn't even like. She doubted Donal much liked it either; he had stayed at the clean end when she was giving birth to the children.

A hard *kaa* sound then a slow inhalation came from the next table. Noreen had fallen asleep. Giuseppe held the almond-scented oil above Therese's scars, red lines like biro marks, above the scraps of skin that held her heart in, some ribbed with silver, some tanned, all cut from her. She nodded.

Back in the hotel, Therese decided against a full shower, wanting to leave the oil on her body. She washed her hair over the bathroom basin. When she came out, Noreen was waiting with a drink. Therese took a sip. Her stomach heaved. Since the surgery, she had only been drunk once, on the night of the pink champagne. Noreen held her glass up.

Here's to getting away. And to Gepetto and his wandering hands.

Giuseppe. And I can't believe you just put me through that.

You loved it.

Feck off.

Thanks for coming with me. I go on holiday by myself no bother, but it's nice not having to.

In the past Therese had pitied Noreen, the diet she started every Monday, the framed inspirational quotes she hung on her walls. Now she saw she had no right. Being alone wasn't the worst thing. It's great Donal doesn't mind you going off by yourself, said Noreen.

Makes no odds to him. It's during term time.

Dishy Donal.

He hadn't put 'dishy' in his profile. Cultured. Sensitive. Discreet. The three words her husband used to describe himself. To make other women want to fuck him.

They changed clothes and put on make-up. They took a taxi around the corner to a restaurant. It was quiet with warm lighting. Therese took the wine list from the waiter. She chose the most expensive white; she was in the habit now of wasting money, flaunting the silliness at Donal. He could hardly object.

She had discovered his purchase by accident. She rarely looked at their bank account. They didn't have a big mortgage, and their salaries, after a slashing at the start of the downturn, had stabilised. There was even a little to spare, so neatly had they been living. Donal persuaded Therese to buy a new car. She wondered now if guilt had made him want to spoil her. Or perhaps it was a diversionary tactic, that she might not notice his

€500 transaction if other new payments were going out. But he had entered one extra digit on the car payment plan and the first instalment had bounced. Therese saw the other payment and contacted Visa to report an error. The boy at the end of the phone asked her to hold while he checked. When he came back on he was tactful. Later, when she clicked on the site and found Donal's profile, she replayed the conversation in her head and heard amusement in the boy's voice. How stupid she must have sounded. *There must be some mistake. No one from this house would be on a site like that.*

Plates of food were carried past them to a table of local men, plump globe artichokes with a little pot of something on the side that smelled lemony, astringent. It wasn't on the menu. The waiter recommended some traditional dishes. They both ordered a *briq*, a pouch of papery pastry filled with crab and egg. Noreen babbled ceaselessly, managing to finish her starter before Therese began hers, and drink most of the wine. Their *couscous royale* arrived. It was served in green and yellow pottery bowls, with a darkly spicy red paste on the side and a jug of broth. Noreen shook the empty bottle at the waiter. They were the only people in the room who were drinking alcohol. He brought two fresh glasses with the wine and asked who would like to taste.

Lob it in there, boss. We'll soon tell you if there's something wrong with it, said Noreen.

He was trying to be professional, but Noreen was pushing the clean glasses back at him. He poured wine from the new bottle into their greasy glasses and left it in the cooler. Noreen took a long drink. Jesus! she said so loudly the waiter rushed across the room.

Madame?

Mademoiselle. It's rank.

I am so sorry. This is why I like to make the proper service.

Serv-eece? she said. It has nothing to do with the serveece that you're selling gone-off wine.

I will bring another bottle.

Don't bother, said Noreen. I'm sickened now.

The other diners had stopped talking. There was no need to speak to him like that, Therese hissed across the table at her. It was like dealing with a child. Not that Therese's daughters would ever be so rude. Not in front of her, at any rate. Maybe they behaved badly when she wasn't looking, like their father.

They paid the bill and hailed a taxi on the street. Noreen said they were going clubbing. End of. Therese could not even imagine what that might mean in Tunisia on a wet Tuesday in March. In the hotel foyer, they followed signs for Pepe's Nite Club along a corridor. The place was huge and empty. The barman clapped his hands together.

What would the beautiful ladies like to drink tonight?

Therese asked for a Coke.

You'd be better off with something clean. Like vodka, said Noreen.

He gave them the cocktail list. It was full of misspelled sexual innuendo. Therese began to panic that Noreen would order her a drink with a pornographic name and leave her to claim it from the barman, so she went to a table and sat down. Noreen danced across the floor to her.

This is gas, isn't it? she said.

The DJ left his box. He walked towards them, one hip swinging wide as he moved, as though one leg was shorter than the other.

Do you mind if I join you? he said.

Therese minded very much.

Feel free, said Noreen. She took off her cardigan, revealing a floral maxi dress. A necklace with her name on it was partly buried in her clothes, a gold NO flashing in the disco lights. Everything else about her said yes.

The barman brought a tray of drinks. Sex on the Beach for two, he said. His name was Kamal.

Noreen prattled away gamely. The weather was a nightmare, but you'd see worse at home. The local food was delicious, but the wine! The hammam was so relaxing. The men looked at each other.

We're going on a trip tomorrow, said Noreen.

Oh? said Kamal.

To Carthage. And Sidi Bou Said.

The DJ said his name was Joe. The barman called him Youssef. He was twenty-two. The lighting made him look older, defining his nose, shading his temple and jawline. He told Therese he had green eyes. She didn't know where to look.

The cocktail was so sweet her teeth were tingling. Joe offered her a cigarette. She put one in her mouth and Noreen screaked. You shouldn't be smoking.

No one should be smoking.

You really shouldn't, said Noreen. Therese had cancer last year. She did great with the surgery. She had one of them off. No chemo, though. Very lucky.

Stop, said Therese. Joe sparked a lighter under the cigarette. The smoke tasted revolting.

Me and Therese used to work together, said Noreen. I had to take leave of absence to look after my mother. Daddy died last year. We had an *annus horribilis*. She pronounced it anus.

You fucking eejit, Therese said softly. Noreen began to laugh.

Joe went back to the DJ box. He put on a slow song. Noreen roared 'unbreak my heart' when the chorus started. Kamal went back to the bar and sloshed the contents of the ice bucket into the sink.

I'd say that pair are looking for the bonk, said Noreen as the song faded out.

They couldn't wait to get away from us.

Fuck them. C'mere, are you glad we did that today?

Not really. I wasn't expecting to have to show the world my mutilation.

It was only me. And the wee man with the bucket. And I'm sure Gepetto has seen worse.

Thanks.

Seen it all, I mean.

Noreen lifted her glass to her lips. Some of the drink didn't make it and dripped from her chin. She wiped the back of her hand across her mouth, leaving her cheek and knuckles glistering with lip gloss. I was so looking forward to this holiday, she said.

Me too, said Therese. It wasn't true. She had come to annoy Donal. She had begun withholding from him, denying him, in the hope it would make him feel as wretched as she did. Pathetic, really. There wasn't much point in withholding yourself from someone who didn't want you. The afternoon had been bizarre. A scrawny youth dressed like an eighties Roger Moore had touched her new breast, groped it and rubbed it because she had paid him to. He had scarcely drizzled oil over her when she became tearful. The skin was numb and monstrous beneath his fingers. I'm afraid of hurting you, Donal had said to her. She hadn't been able to tell him that there was no sensation. It was dead, like a hide. In the months that followed they grew shy with each other. She thought it would pass. Then the car payment bounced.

When he came home from work that night she was waiting at the kitchen table. She had drunk the best part of a bottle of pink champagne, a get-well present. Later she regretted her choice of drink. Whiskey or brandy would have given the proceedings some gravitas. The confrontation was exhilarating. She had found herself online too, she told him. Oh yes. She had gone online to find out why. *Cosmopolitan* told her it was meaningless, that loads of middle-aged men watched porn and preferred sex with strangers. As she was reading, ads for sex toys and vibrators had flashed at her. And you know what? She might buy some, because it wasn't up to much, in fairness, that side of it, when she had to squash him in because he was a bit wishy-washy in that department. It was intoxicating, getting to say anything and everything she had ever wanted to say. And there was so much, wasn't there, that you could say to someone who had given up their right to fight back? Someone who stood in front of you full of a shame you could hardly bear to behold, because you were full of shame yourself.

She had tried to calm down. In fairness, she said, she didn't blame him. It must be so dreary being married to her at the best of times. And now, with her Frankenstein boob and sensible clothes. To be honest, she wouldn't mind being ridden sideways by someone new, a young fella with a langer you could hang a coat on. But in fairness, in fucking fairness, she would be actually embarrassed to put herself out there. As for the words he used to describe himself. Ha! Cultured. Sensitive! Discreet? Such a laugh, she said. Only she didn't feel like laughing because she didn't think anything would ever be the same again and even though he had only set up the account, and there was no activity on it, and she could see he had tried to close it, it was too late. He had wanted to go elsewhere and now he could fuck away off elsewhere and into the spare room, where he still slept.

Noreen finished her drink and crossed the empty dance floor in the direction of the toilets. Therese followed her. She was in a cubicle, the door jammed open by her backside. Therese held her hair out of her face until she had finished retching.

I'm fucking twisted.

Therese leaned over her and pressed the flusher. Come on. We haven't far to go.

When they came out Joe was gone. Kamal jiggled a bunch of keys until they were through the door. Noreen reeled between the walls on the way to the room. At the sight of her bed, she hurtled on to it in her clothes. Therese covered her with a bedspread and left a glass of water on the locker beside her.

There was a rap at the door. Joe was in the corridor, wearing a leather jacket.

I didn't say goodnight, he said. His eyes were green, all right.

After he left Therese went out on the balcony. It had stopped raining. The flooding on the asphalt had begun to drop and the wind was down. She sat for a long time and watched the deserted street, night fading to dawn. There was a text from Donal. The kids had got hold of his phone and sent those daft messages. Her poor girls. They had taken to coming into her bed in the mornings, asking why their father was in the other room. If there was anything more shameful than getting a knee-trembler off a young fella in a hotel corridor, it was the idea of her daughters trying to make things right.

She was showered and ready by eight. She read the train timetable once more, memorising where to change for the other line that would bring them along the coast.

She shook Noreen's shoulder. Shift yourself, she said. Our train's at eight forty.

Noreen heaved on to her side. I'm in rag order. And I've enough of looking at ruins living with the mother.

Therese threw a sachet of Alka Seltzer at her. What'll you do for the day?

I might go back to the hammam. See what the story is with that Gepetto fella.

Therese walked to the station. It was dull, but there was warmth in the sky that seemed to promise sunshine. She sat by a window, relieved to be in transit, rattling away from the resort. She changed at Tunis, taking a path through a dilapidated part of town and boarding a train at another station. Noreen would have hated it. After a few stops, apartment blocks and auto repair stores thinned to show glimpses of scrub-covered dirt, flashes of sea. The carriage was full, a party of French students taking up the rest of the seats. When the train arrived at Carthage she let them get off ahead of her. She waited until they had joined the queues and walked to where she had a clear view of the pale green sea. The seam of cloud had begun to break up. Weak sunlight slanted across the stone. The ruins were laid out in front of her, pooled with rainwater that glittered like crystals of salt.

WHAT THE BIRDS HEARD

The birds hear her first. Light beats of their wings and the tern rise, seven or eight of them, a few feet above the mudflat, before fluttering back down. Doireann thinks about walking on, but Tim Gallagher pauses, seems to listen. He is just below the path, on the bank of the estuary, in a structure like a garden shed that is missing a wall. He taps in a tack and speaks without looking up.

You're late today, he says, as though she has kept him waiting. She goes down the grassy bank. It's steep, and she finds herself slithering fast. At the bottom, he steps out of the shed and catches her by the upper arm, letting go when she's steady.

I was answering emails, she says, loath to admit she woke tired and went back to bed with a mug of tea. Three glassless windows have been cut into the side of the shed that overlooks the estuary. The fresh timber has a mossy smell she finds sickening. What's this going to be? she asks.

It's for birdwatching, he says, stepping aside to let her in. The windows are different sizes, at different heights, one low, for a child. He bends to a holdall, a khaki canvas one from an army surplus store, and takes out a set of binoculars, unwrapping the strap. There is something boyish and unselfconscious in the act that makes her feel tender towards him. She is annoyed at herself. Put the cord round your neck, he says, they're heavy.

The binoculars have been cast in a metal like beaten aluminium and are cold and rough to the touch. These are so old, says Doireann.

They came off a U-boat.

No way.

The German submarine fleet surrendered into Derry at the end of the war, he says. His accent is strongest when he says the name of his home town.

Through the lenses, she looks across the estuary to the north pier. A small boat is listing on its side at the end of the slipway, its flaking hull dipping in the water. There are other birds she doesn't recognise on the far bank. What are those ones called? The ones with the call like a cry.

You're supposed to watch and listen, then go home and look them up. She lingers, wanting him to say more, but he's picked up the hammer and is turning away.

Do you want to come over for dinner? she says.

Yeah.

See you later, then. She plucks a blossom from a meadowsweet stalk and rubs at it, releasing its almond musk. The sound of Tim Gallagher's hammer rings around the estuary as she walks away, each faint tap-tap followed by a pause as he picks up a tack and positions it. She wonders if he looks her way, even for a second, and feels silly for the indulgence. She manages not to look back.

She loves these silty flats best at low tide, when the river seems to have been sucked from its bed. At the dry mouth she turns on to the shore, gathering pace when she reaches the firm tidal sand that can hold her footing. The moment the bank bends to meet the beach never fails to surprise her, the rush of white and wind. She hasn't figured out how to tell what the sea is doing, whether it's coming or going, and has forgotten to bring the book of tides he gave her.

She hadn't intended to come so far north. After she left Paul, she had wanted to move west, to Louisburgh or Roundstone or Ballyvaughan, but the cottage was cheap and available for a year, with a conservatory she could use as a studio. The other neighbours came to say hello the day she moved in. She passed Tim Gallagher's house several times before he spoke to her. She was on her way to the beach. It was just after eight, the morning bright then suddenly dull when clouds came in.

I hope you don't get the weather you're expecting, he said. He was putting resin on an old surfboard, swiping it with long strokes. He was wearing a sleeveless wetsuit, a mottling of sun damage on his shoulders and arms. From a distance he had looked tanned.

It might rain.

You've all the gear, anyway.

She had bought expensive outdoor clothing online and it hadn't lost the brand-new look. Oh God, she said. I'm like a German tourist, aren't I?

Ja. Or a nordie pensioner.

I'll be here for the winter, so I thought I should get kitted out.

You think you'll last the winter, he said, more observation than question. He turned the surfboard over and began buffing it with a cloth. She looked around. Her cottage had been gentrified, the front door painted a shade of lavender, the small garden planted with blue-green grasses and pink carnations and delphiniums. His place was a mess. A crab apple tree bent away from the wind, gnarled branches spindled around themselves. Chunks of splintered driftwood, not propped against walls or laid across window ledges, but thrown randomly around the grass. Clumps of netting and plastic crates from the fishery, a trailer stacked with surfboards. An avocado-coloured plastic bath filled with wetsuits, a hose slung over its side, water dribbling towards the road. He dropped the cloth on the ground and looked at her sidelong. You've settled in, then?

I haven't figured the telly out, which is probably for the best. I'm getting loads of work done.

What work would that be?

She told him about her studio at the back of the cottage. How she works every day from one of the hundreds of photographs taken at the estuary on her phone. That she paints on pages torn from an Edwardian *Encyclopaedia of Birds*, a lone guillemot or pipit or kingfisher. That an interiors magazine said the range was 'ideal for vintage-smitten bird nerds', how that was fine because she had known before she finished art college her work was mediocre and had done a Data Science postgrad. That she hadn't known how much she had missed painting until she moved here. That for her it was about the process, the search for the right shade for a beak or feather, the smudging and blurring. He looked from her mouth to her eyes while she spoke. She fell silent, fretting she had sounded gushy, and waited for him to say something. He appeared to feel no obligation to reply. She decided he was rude and turned to go.

I could have a gander at it, I suppose, he said.

What?

The telly. I might have a look at it.

She shrugged and went down to the beach. She remembered who he reminded her of and sent a message to her sister. *Just met the most eligible bachelor in Inishowen.*

Pushing fifty and sporting a sleeveless wetsuit that made him look like the Only Gay in the Village.

He came to the cottage just after seven, when she was about to eat. He looked at the place she had set for herself at the table, the glass of wine. Very posh, he said.

Do you want a glass? said Doireann. He didn't answer, which she was getting used to. He took the two remote controls and began waving them at the television and pressing buttons. She turned the gas off under her dinner and pretended to wash the dishes. He showed her how to switch the television on and off, how to change channels and set recordings. She thanked him and stood near the door to see him out.

Were you not threatening to give me a drink? he said.

She took the bottle from the fridge. He rested his backside against the sink and watched her pour. I made a pot of something, if you haven't eaten, she said.

Can't have you horsing into a pot of something all by yourself, I suppose.

It was a navarin of lamb, enough for a few days. She told him she had made the stew with hogget from the butcher in Malin Village who only stocked meat from his own flocks, and carrots and leeks and turnips from the man who sold from a van outside the secondary school in Carndonagh on Saturday mornings. Paul had liked to talk about what they ate, using words like provenance and even, towards the end, terroir. Tim Gallagher gave her a look she couldn't read and held his plate out for more.

Three evenings later he brought turf. Last year's, nice and dry, he told her; he was making room in his shed for freshly cut stuff. He came and went, slinging five fertiliser bags of it against the side of the front porch. He washed his hands at the kitchen sink then walked around her sitting room, picking things up, looking at them. He went into the conservatory. A page was pegged to the drawing board, the outline of a cormorant marked in fine pencil. She thought she gleaned approval in how he leaned in for a closer look.

She had bought a litre of Powers when she moved in, imagining her neighbours calling in for a drink, as if they were all characters in a John McGahern book. She offered him a hot whiskey. They drank the bottle. He put down his glass and looked at her, his eyes creasing. It was supposed to be a smile. She almost laughed; he was more plausible when he was being unpleasant. She stood to bring the glasses to the sink and the room tilted. I'm plastered, she said.

Tim Gallagher swallowed. Do you want to lie down? he said.

The fucking, for there is no other word for it, happens at her cottage. He brings an offering, leaving it on the table rather than presenting it to her. Lemon geranium cuttings, a jar of crab apple jelly, a salmon that he gutted and portioned for her. It gives their couplings shades of *meitheal*, as if it's an exchange of labour, a neighbourly effort. When he brings wine, it is from one of the English supermarkets in Derry, big Spanish and Italian reds that are almost expensive, but they don't drink much. It's better when they're sober. When he speaks, the words are short ones. There. More. Wait. Now. Yeah. Now. They utter no endearments, are not seen together in public. When she runs into him in the village he is reserved, even unfriendly. So is Doireann, although once in the pub she became distracted when he took a first sip from his pint. She had a flashback to the previous night, when he had pulled her breast free of the stiff cup of her bra and lapped at her nipple.

When she and Paul were trying for a baby, sex was drudgery. She could scarcely cope with the schedule, for that was what he called it, when she was ovulating. Worse was to come, when his GP told him they needed to have sex throughout the month. Loads of sex. Paul bought a Nutribullet and fed her shots of foul green slime at dawn. Grim-faced, he mounted her morning and night, pumping at her joylessly, insisting that she latch on *till she got all of it*, a task she found as erotic as wringing out a floorcloth. One night, he told her he had read on the Internet that if he held her legs up afterwards it would increase the chances of fertilisation. She cried and said if he could inseminate her like a cow he would. He didn't contradict her.

Monthly, Doireann endured Paul's disappointment at the sight of a tampon wrapper. The pained look on his face when his mother asked if there was any news and muttered that PJ, God rest him, had only to throw his trousers on the bed to put six of them in her, one after the other. Doireann grew to despise the need in Paul, the frustrated vanity. How he said she was enough for him, though they both knew it wasn't true. She told him she needed a break, just for a few weeks, but hadn't anticipated the relief she would feel when she strapped herself into her car and put her small case on the passenger seat. Or the elation when she withdrew their IVF fund from the Credit Union and ran away.

Now she lies down with Tim Gallagher. She makes light of it. *How's the booty call?* asks her sister. *LOL* replies Doireann, without laughing. She dismisses the thing with him, whatever it is, to herself. When he goes to Derry she frets he is seeing a woman there and has to slap the thought down. What if he is? He isn't her boyfriend. This is meaningless, functional. Isn't it?

She clambers up on to the dunes. Deep in the marram grass, little things witter and fuss. She stumbles, her boot finding itself snug in a rabbit hole; sidesteps vetch and bee orchid, wild carrot and fennel. Tiny birds trill, unseen and nervy, as though she has triggered an alarm. She takes out her phone and opens the camera app, tilting and clicking, trying to catch the shadows the clouds cast as they move in from the sea.

Down on to the shore again, across the black rocks. The wind is behind her, the tide washing in. At the end of the beach, she goes up the concrete path and into the playground. Twin girls in yellow anoraks are screaming to be pushed on the swings at the same time. Their knackered-looking mother raises her eyes to the skies and smirks at Doireann, who finds herself smiling back.

She's on the path again, can hear the faint tap-tap of Tim Gallagher's hammer. A gull screaks overhead, an awful sound that goes through her. For the last couple of weeks, everything has felt heightened, the grasses scratching at her, spits of rain needling her skin. She pauses above the wooden hut. Tim Gallagher is kneeling on the fresh timber, opening a tin of creosote. If he knows she's there, he doesn't let on. A gust of wind takes the breath from her, and she feels a flutter, a quickening in her belly. She puts her head down and keeps walking.

Her cottage is untidy. On the kitchen windowsill there is a bowl of razor clam shells that she might use to frame a mirror or photograph. Books and notes are stacked on the table. There is something hopeful about the clutter, as if it might become something better. She makes tea and brings it to the conservatory. At her desk, she loads the images from her phone on to her computer, swiping through them slowly. As usual, they are disappointing.

Every day she tries to capture the palette of the coast-line, the soft, ever-morphing hues, in thrall to light and hour and water. But there's no way to catch the heat of the sun on her face, or the hiss of the wind.

She pins paper to the board and traces the lines of the hut, working outwards to add the wide, dry bed of the estuary. She hasn't attempted a seascape since college, and it takes most of the day to lay down the bones of it. At four, she goes to the kitchen. She opens the fridge door and instantly dry-retches. There's a wrap of goat's cheese on the shelf that she had planned on crumbling over pasta. She normally loves the smell of it, but today it seems sharp and chemical, like ammonia. She takes it outside and puts it in the bin. Pregnant women aren't supposed to eat unpasteurised cheese and, according to the four plastic wands she's hidden in the bathroom, she is a pregnant woman.

She lays cherry tomatoes on a tray and daubs them with butter and salt and thyme. While they're roasting, she makes fresh pasta, hanging the floury ribbons on the backs of the kitchen chairs. There is always something performative in her preparations for him, as if she's setting a scene. Tim Gallagher only cooked for her once, an invi-tation he seemed to regret by the time she arrived. She complimented him on the table and he looked mortified. He took down a wine glass from a dusty shelf, running a finger around it to remove a dead fly, and was vexed when she didn't want to drink from it. He wouldn't let her help, and she had sat at his table, sipping from the dirty glass. Around the room there were clumps of hydrangea and sunflowers and honesty drying in make-shift vases, and each time he dropped turf on the fire he swept the hearth briskly. He cooked with a Family Circle biscuit tin open beside him in which he keeps herbs and spices and stock cubes, and when he filled the kettle or peeled vegetables, there was grace and economy in his movements. It was almost unbearable to watch; something gentle, almost feminine, in how he moved around his house, a man used to ministering to himself.

When he isn't around, she replays their intimacies in her head. The way he pushes the heel of his hand along her breastbone towards her throat. The small tight sound that comes from the back of his tongue as he finishes. How she can't reconcile the way he touches her with the way he dismisses her. The less he gives her the more she wants.

She changes into a cotton dress, dark grey with tiny white daisies. Her breasts have swollen and it's snug at the bodice, where it used to gape. She applies mascara and brushes her hair and sits on the couch to wait for him. He comes at seven, like he always does, rapping the door twice with his knuckles and letting himself in. She gets to her feet. He's looking at the pasta on the chairs, irritation passing over his face at having nowhere to sit.

She fetches a bowl and begins lifting the noodles away.
She wishes he'd kiss her.

Nice frock, he says, but you'd want to watch yourself.

Why?

Women with tits like yours often run to fat. He tosses
his jacket on to the couch and goes into the conservatory. Doireann looks at the table; he hasn't brought
anything. She follows, standing behind him as he exam-
ines the drawing. She's left a blank space in the hut, the
hunched shape of him as he bent to take the binoculars
from his bag. It's hard to tell whether she has erased him
or intends to add him later.

She pours him a glass of wine and he stands by her,
watching her cook. She mashes anchovies with a fork
and stirs them into the collapsed tomatoes, adds more
butter, twists of pepper. It makes her feel housewifey.

He eats with a frown on his face, lifting hefty forkfuls
to his mouth and chewing rhythmically.

Do you like it? she says.

Yeah.

It's all he'll give her.

In the bedroom, she crosses her arms and lifts the dress
over her head. She gets under the covers and watches
him take off his clothes. He removes each item slowly,
draping his shirt and trousers over the back of the Lloyd
Loom chair in the corner, pairing his socks into a woolly
egg shape. He sits on the edge of the bed.

This room freaks me out, he says.

What do you mean?

Fucking presses in on me. Like being in a womb.

For a moment, she thinks he's going to leave, but he draws back the quilt. His hands and mouth are on her then, until she's sopping.

When she wakes, he's gone. She looks at the other side of the bed for some sign he was here, but the pillow is smooth and full, as if it hasn't been slept on. He didn't stay long enough to leave an impression on it. She gets up and pulls the dress over her naked body. She walks through the kitchen barefoot, crumbs of pasta dough sticking to her feet, and goes to the conservatory. She lifts a pencil and adds a flock of tern, wings out, rising, to the drawing. She looks at the hut, at the space she's left for Tim Gallagher, and begins to fill in the interior walls and floor, until there's not even a suggestion of him. He was right. She won't last the winter.

GIBRALTAR

Audrey McGuigan is in front of the wire fence that marks the end of their garden, where newly-planted lawn gives way to tufts of roseroot and marram grass. Behind her, Ben Bulben is under cloud, only the west side visible, curving into the sea. The tide is out, an acrid slime covering the seabed. A dog has left the carcass of a sewage-fattened mullet in the low dunes and the smell repulses her; she is seven months pregnant. Marty hasn't figured out how to use his new camera, and Audrey has been stock-still for five minutes. He's just noticed how huge she is, at least as big as when she was at full term with Rory, who is out of the picture, climbing over the Gibraltar Rocks to get away from his parents' bickering. After a clutch of car sales, Marty goes to auctions. He has bought a scrap of waste ground, a terraced house on Harmony Hill, a derelict shop near the docks. He also bought the field that borders Gibraltar. Half an hour ago, he put a sign on one of the gates that reads KEEP OFF

THESE LANDS. Where is he going with his lands, Audrey wanted to know, and him reared in Belubah bloody Terrace. Their Queen Anne-style house is a bespoke pine kitchen away from finished. Rockview Lodge, they'll call it; there will be a row about that too.

1990

This one was taken by a photographer. The parish priest is between Marty and Audrey, delighted to pose with the man who gave him five per cent off a new Mondeo and threw in alloy wheels for nothing. Audrey's mouth is smiling. Her left hand is buried in the cloud of Shona's veil to stop it from blowing away. The Communion dress is cut from Audrey's wedding gown. Shona would have preferred a dress from a shop, but her mother had been so keen to take scissors to the lace and tulle she hadn't said so. Her palms are touching, as if in prayer, a white satin handbag swinging from her wrist that's already bulging with cards and cash and Nanny Lynch's rosary beads. The more you have the more you get, Marty thinks. The day of his own Communion his father poured him a whis-key in the scullery and went out to the pub to celebrate by himself. There's a meal booked in the hotel, where he'll have to buy drinks for everyone in the bar, because that's what is expected when you own half the town and employ the other half. At least it'll give him something to do while Audrey and the children are at the long table, flanked by the Lynches. Rory is in a brown blouson jacket, his right foot raised an inch off the ground, as if he's about to bolt. Audrey would bolt too, given half a chance.

2001

Shona is wearing a one-shouldered purple dress, her long hair straightened, eyebrows thin and arched. She is smiling over at her mother while Marty takes the picture. The boy beside her is called Keith and has a blond ponytail and a bar through his eyebrow. His handshake is limp and Marty thinks Shona should think more of herself and find someone else. Not that he will say so. He and Shona aren't that close. Keith has been making a particular contribution to Shona's low self-esteem. A couple of shoves, what the counsellor will later call verbal abuse, and the previous night a smack that cut through the fug of hash in her bedroom.

2011

The florist has erected a bower of pink peonies and unripe wheat and white rhododendrons at the end of the garden, on the exact spot where Marty photographed Audrey with Shona in her belly. The family are in front of it, Marty and Audrey on either side of the bride and groom, Rory and the English girl he lives with in New Zealand (South

Island, as far away from Rockview as you can get) beside Audrey, yet slightly apart. Shona's hair is set in loose waves. She has just married Lorcan, an eejity fella, in Marty's opinion, but an improvement on that weasel Keith. They have been blessed with the weather. Not that it matters, because there's thirty grand's worth of a marquee with a merbau floor and chandeliers and vintage china teapots filled with cornflowers and anemones. Audrey is wearing oyster-coloured georgette. Her wig is a toffee shade that almost suits her, although it feels like a bathing hat she had as a child, a pink rubber abomination with flaccid flowers. Marty is preoccupied. He's not a man for speeches. He'll talk about how beautiful Shona looks. He'll say how happy he is to welcome Lorcan to the family, that he had better be good to Shona or he'll have him to answer to, and everyone will laugh. (He isn't joking on this front, as Keith with the bar in his eyebrow would attest.) The rest he'll keep to himself. That he would not have believed you could love a child that wasn't yours until Shona's arms were reaching up at him, demanding to be carried. How hard it was to give the love in the first place. How very much harder not to give it.

1980

Audrey's hair is cut in a pageboy style, her fringe full and bouncy. She is wearing a light blouse with shoulder pads, and a Black Watch kilt over leather boots. There's a pair of scissors in her hand. The tape she has just cut hasn't yet touched the ground and looks as though it's swirling about her, like the ribbons gymnasts dance with. Behind them are two brand-new Ford Sierras, all curvy windows and bubbly lines. They will be recalled in a few months because of a fault with the carburettor, and Marty will almost lose the business for the first time. His suit is loose at the waist, the creases in his trousers sharp.

The photograph was a centrefold in the local paper, other businesses placing an advert around it to congratulate them on the new showroom. The one on the bottom right is for the legal practice where Audrey works part-time. 'Wishing Audrey and Marty all the very best' it read, the Mullen & Kilcoyne logo bent over a drawing of the scales of justice.

1983

Treasa Callaghan is holding the camera and has already appointed herself godmother.

Audrey is propped against pillows holding Shona Bridget McGuigan, who arrived at 11:04 a.m. while Marty was in the Innisfree Cafeteria beside the hospital chapel, moving pieces of currant scone around a plate. Shona is a fine child, nine pounds four ounces. A remarkable weight for a baby who arrived five weeks early. Bridie Lynch has swung one ample bum cheek on to the bed and is regarding the pair suspiciously. She may have left school at fourteen, but she knows when her daughter is trying to hide something. Audrey is watching Marty, who is out of the frame. He's sitting on the windowsill, looking down over the town. To the west the sky is almost black, a cold blue to the east. Three watery rainbows are arching over the town, over the fairy fort in front of his mother's council house, over the crow's nest on the old Polloxfen building, over the mock-Gothic tower of the Court House. Unless you counted the night of the Chamber of Commerce AGM, he hasn't been near Audrey in over a year, and even then he hardly put a hand on her. He had come in quietly and sat up against the headboard until an antacid tablet started to work on the reflux caused by his hiatus hernia. She had climbed on to him without a word and by some trick of her thumb and finger taken him in, rocking in his lap until he filled her. It was like having sex with someone else. Not that he has ever had sex with anyone else. Audrey wishes they'd all just go, so she can figure out where the payphone is and try calling Matt Kilcoyne again.

1976

There's a heatwave. A wedding car is parked to the right of the cathedral. The rear passenger door is open and

Audrey is waiting, fishtail train spread across the melting tarmac, lace almost blue in the implausible sunlight. Treasa Callaghan is meant to be holding the train, but the head bridesmaid is eleven feet away, up on her toes, her mouth to Marty's ear. Marty is looking at the wedding car. Treasa Callaghan has just told him Audrey is wearing a baby-blue garter under her dress. Later in the hotel in Westport, when he puts his trembling hand up her satin nightgown, he'll feel a ruched rash on Audrey's thigh, where the elastic has eaten into her skin in the heat. She'll flinch, but he'll be so nervous about finding the right hole he won't ask if she's all right or think about the garter again until forty years later when he sees this photograph.

1986

In homage to *Jungle Book*, Shona is naked except for a fat nappy and a banana skin that is opened on her bobbed hair. She is lying across Marty's chest, her cheek against his. Marty knows the exact date on which this photograph was taken. 22nd June 1986, the Sunday of the Connaught final. Galway beat Roscommon 1–8 to 1–5. He missed the first half to let Shona finish watching her video; Shona is a daddy's girl. Only three people know Marty isn't her daddy. He is fairly confident about that, because he called out to Matt Kilcoyne's house in the

Lower Rosses the day Shona was born. It didn't take much to warn him off, which had annoyed Marty; the wee rat could at least have fought for them. On the way back up to the hospital, though, he fretted briefly that he might have just kicked Matt Kilcoyne's bollocks into his mouth.

The photograph is an instant Polaroid. Audrey takes it and waves it in the air, watching them, watching her child pressing against a man who isn't her father, trying to mesmerise him with a rendition of 'Trust in Me'. Audrey gave up her job in Mullen & Kilcoyne Solicitors after Shona was born. She was only working to get her out of the house, she told anyone who asked. Matt Kilcoyne BL is engaged to a 24-year-old A&E nurse from Longford. It has been almost three years, yet some days the loss of him weighs so heavy on her she can scarcely breathe.

2016

Audrey is holding up a glass of champagne. Her navy cashmere cardigan is flattering to the jaundiced tint of her skin, the white hair that has begun to fur her scalp since they stopped her treatment. Shona says she looks like Jamie Lee Curtis, who Marty has never heard of. Lorcan is holding Amber Mae, who is two, dark-haired and earnest like her mother. Shona looks tired, her pregnant belly only a little fuller than her mother's distended abdomen. Marty is beside Audrey, his arm stretched out behind her, close but not touching. Rory left for New Zealand three days ago. He has split up from the English girl, who won't give him access to their son.

This photo is Shona's favourite. She is going to put it in the Mass leaflet. She wants the funeral to be a celebration of her mother's life. Shona has planned a party for afterwards, a buffet with tables in the garden and large prints of family photos around the house. Marty would settle for a meal in the hotel, but doesn't say so. The last few years at Rockview have been almost happy. Like visiting some other couple, Shona has told Lorcan. They'll send Audrey off from here.

1973

Audrey is behind her mother, on a slab of rock. She is wearing a white halter-neck dress and has tied a navy-and-white striped scarf around her hair. She is holding sunglasses in her right hand and looking at the camera. Not smiling, just looking. Marty is out of the frame to the right. He goes to Gibraltar at high tide twice a week to bathe in the tidal pool the council constructed in 1951; the houses on his street were built without bathrooms. He has taken off his shirt and is aware of the ruddy skin that rings his neck and forearms, the startling pale of his torso. He is close enough to see that Audrey has a black bubbly mole just under her left shoulder blade, raised and horny, like a woodlouse. He wonders what would happen if he ran his finger across it, if it would yield to his touch or stay raised. The colour in the photo has both faded and brightened to give everything a tint you never saw then or since. Marty can confirm that the mole stayed hard when you pressed it, though. And that, in the early days, Audrey Lynch had quite liked the feel of his fingers on her back.

POWDER

Eithne glanced at the passenger seat, expecting Sandy to be asleep. The woman had to be exhausted. She had travelled to Dublin from Ohio through the night, a ninety-mile car ride and two flights. But Sandy was wide awake, sitting very straight, clutching her bulging handbag close to her chest. It occurred to Eithne that Ethan's ashes were not in the big red suitcase. His mother was holding him in her arms.

Are you hungry, Sandy?

I guess. I haven't eaten since last night. Or I think it was last night.

They stopped at Barack Obama Plaza, a place Ethan had found hilarious. Sandy didn't get the joke. They sat at a plastic table and Sandy lined up her food in front of her, like a child in a school canteen.

We're on the road, Sandy, said Eithne.

Yes we are, said Sandy. A skin was forming on the paper cup of baked beans she had ordered.

You'll love the scenery. Especially if we get the weather, said Eithne. The week was going to be torturous.

Sandy picked up a piece of popcorn chicken. An emaciated, surprised-looking boy with flesh tunnels through his ears sat beside her and emptied four sachets of sugar into his coffee. I wouldn't ate in this place, he said, eyes roving around the room and from one woman to the other, if you fucken paid me. They kill the chickens by throwing them against the wall. Sandy took a wide-eyed suck from her Coke, her expression like the boy's, and ate nothing until breakfast the next day.

Since then they had posed at the Rock of Cashel, kissed the Blarney Stone, idled in Killarney traffic watching shit fall into a leather nappy from the rump of a chestnut pony. From time to time, Eithne searched Sandy's face for a sign of collusion, for a look that said she found it bizarre too, touring Ireland in a rented Nissan Note, doing this most macabre of bucket lists. Americans don't do black humour, Ethan had told her, especially my mother. Sandy sat down to dinner in restaurants, ambled towards lake shores, leaned over cliff edges, all the time clutching her misshapen handbag, and scarcely raised her head to look around her. Months of planning had gone into the trip, but Sandy could have been anywhere.

It wasn't all bad. Sandy had chosen their accommodation from a website, Secret Ireland. They stayed in elegant historic properties, places Eithne could not have afforded. Sandy had booked separate rooms, so after dinner Eithne could get away from her.

On the fourth day they visited the Cliffs of Moher. When they arrived at the castle there was a problem; their rooms had been double-booked. Sandy and Eithne would have to share. The only room left was a twin in a garret, with a mouldy PVC skylight and a water-mark above the toilet in the en suite. Eithne couldn't face spending all evening in the room with Sandy. After dinner she went to the bar alone. She ordered a 'Hedgerow Martini' and sat in a blue-and-gold brocade armchair. The drink smelled of marzipan and tasted like garden compost. Ethan would have enjoyed it – not the flavour, the emperor's-new-clothes aspect of it. He used to order craft beers and rename them. Scaly Brendan's Stagnant Bathwater. Nursing Brigid's Milk Stout.

There were a few couples sitting at tables around the room. The lone man at the counter was tall and expensively dressed. When Eithne's drink was almost gone the barman brought her another. The man got off the stool and smoothed the front of his trousers. He came and stood by her table.

May I? His shirt was crisp, his wedding ring thick and pinkish.

I can hardly say no, can I? She held the glass up and took a long drink. He sat down.

His name was Ross. He was from Chicago. He was direct, in the way Ethan had been. She remembered she had liked being around someone so easy in himself. He was celebrating, he said, and told her about the deal he had signed with a start-up in Shannon. He had a company, a wife, two sons.

In that order? she asked.

It isn't polite to talk about politics, he said, then talked about politics. He paused to let her laugh at his jokes and didn't seem to expect her to say much. On another night this would have annoyed her. Tonight she was enjoying not having to make conversation. With Sandy, she found herself talking incessantly: a continual update on what they were doing, where they were going. Trivial talk; between them, the important words were still unsaid.

Two more drinks arrived. Ross pulled his chair close and stiffened his thigh against hers. The movement was precise, perfunctory. She wondered how many times he had done this. She felt drunk and sad. Sandy was alone upstairs while she was flirting with Ross, Republican Party reptile, who was wearing a shirt so well pressed that it rustled, presumably ironed by his wife. She stood suddenly and tried to blink away the drunken whirl. Ross got up and patted his pockets for room key, mobile phone. How was she going to get out of this one?

After you.

I'm a widow.

Excuse me?

I'm a widow. I'm here with my mother-in-law.

I didn't realise. I'm sorry ...

She fled upstairs.

She was out of breath when she got to the room. Sandy was sitting up in bed, the handbag in her lap. Without her make-up her face was delicate, papery.

Jesus, Sandy. You weren't waiting up for me, were you?

Sometimes it takes a while for me to fall asleep.

Eithne went to the bathroom. She locked the door and looked in the mirror. Her roots were greasy, violet under-eye circles showing where her concealer had worn off. If Sandy hadn't been in the next room she would have made herself vomit.

Fucking get it together, she told her reflection. She went back into the bedroom, in time to see Sandy tilting pills from her palm into her mouth. Eithne got into bed, turned her back and switched off her lamp.

Goodnight, Eithne.

Goodnight, Sandy.

Goodnight, Mary Ellen.

Very funny, Ethan, she murmured, and fell asleep. She woke just after three with a headache, hedgerow aromatics gurgling in her bowels. For the rest of the night she lay awake. Her shame deepened with each Ativan-thickened breath from the other bed.

Breakfast was served by the barman from the previous night. He was discreet and professional, like the brochure promised. When Ross came in, he seated him at a table near the window. Still, what if he came over, offered condolences to them? A flush rose from her neck to her cheeks. As for the food, Sandy had ordered her eggs 'sunny side up' and was stabbing the oily yolk with the tip of her knife. Eithne pushed her plate away and went outside for a cigarette. The secrets people kept, the lies they told. And she was no better. How was she going to get through the week?

Yet she did. They had Guinness and oysters by a weir in Clarinbridge and spent a night in Galway city. They took the road from Leenane to Louisburgh and caught a ferry to Clare Island. If Sandy was vague and distracted, she was also polite and charming. Wherever they went the staff loved her. Eithne didn't feel the need to talk so much and once or twice had to admit to herself she was having fun.

On the way to Inishowen they visited Yeats's grave. It was windy, the shelf of Ben Bulben blurred by low cloud. Some of the older graves were overhung with pink hydrangeas. Even Sandy was captivated.

They reckon they reinterred the wrong bones. Louis MacNeice said they buried a Frenchman with a club foot, said Eithne, reading from her phone. Sandy looked appalled. The black-humour thing again.

For their final night they arrived at a dowager house at the end of a long avenue choked by woodland. A balding man in his fifties greeted them. Hey ho. Is there a dead body in here? he said, using a knee and both hands to get the red case out of the boot. He staggered ahead of them. His name was Redmond O'Neill. He gave a short history of the house, of *the family*, and joked about Victorian plumbing as he panted up the stairs.

When Eithne had come here with Ethan in the winter they stayed at the golf resort, a vanity project built by a developer who had long since fled. She hated the mock-Georgian facade, the purple-and-taupe bar area that could have been in Birmingham or Riga or Perth. They walked to the village for a pint. Paint flaked from the closed door of the only pub, a price list in punts bleached almost blank in the window.

She was glad Sandy had chosen this old house. There was a gravity about it, with its dark furniture and drab oil portraits of unsmiling men in Victorian dress, although it too was changing. A famous sportsman had married a starlet here the previous Easter. Features on it had begun to appear in Sunday supplements and fashion magazines. Now the quietly rich who had enjoyed it for years found themselves at the communal table in the evenings in the company of Americans doing Europe and thirty-some-things from Dublin who changed for dinner. People like Sandy and Eithne.

She paused on the turn of the staircase to put her bag in her other hand. She felt a heave of dread that they would have to share a room again. They crossed the landing on to a wide corridor with a bow window at the far end. A rusty dappling from a rowan tree flickered across the carpet. It felt as though the house was rising out of the damp wood.

Your mother has the best room in the house, said Redmond.

Oh, she's not my mother, said Eithne. She sounded cheerful. She blushed.

Eithne and my son were engaged, said Sandy. Redmond took in her use of the past tense. He let her words settle then pushed open a door. Sandy's room was enormous, with a four-poster bed hung with heavy tuberose-patterned linen, and views of a fast river lined by sallies and yellow irises. They arranged to meet in the lobby at three. Redmond led Eithne to a room at the end of the corridor. It had a high, narrow bed covered with a quilt in shades of kingfisher and royal blue, a tiny chaise longue under a tall window. After he left, she lay on the bed and flicked through the welcome pack, a folder of fliers for walks and attractions in the area, bound in faux leather. She had done some of them with Ethan. Now she would have to do them with Sandy. She closed her eyes. One more night. She had endured Ethan's death, and his funeral. Surely she could do this?

Eithne had met Ethan on a team-building weekend in Connemara; Plex.com liked its staff to socialise. Ethan had just arrived from Head Office in Portland, Oregon. He was casually excellent at the activities, most of which she found hateful. She didn't notice him before the trip, but he seemed to be everywhere after it.

Ethan and Eithne, he said when he asked her out the following week. Serendipitous. It's worth a go. The sheer corny cheek of him made her say yes. After a while he extended his contract, kept the shiny apartment the company were paying for at Grand Canal Dock. On week nights she slept over; it was convenient for work. She held on to the tiny terraced house in Phibsboro she had bought when the boom was still getting boomier: a dim cave of bazaar colours and old-lady things, chunky china from the forties and fifties, and G Plan sideboards painted in high-gloss finishes. The spinster house, Ethan called it. They settled into a sort of domesticity, without the routine that might have made it dreary. And then he died.

Eithne went downstairs at ten to three. Sandy was waiting and had changed into a white short-sleeved blouse trimmed with navy anchors, and red polyester trousers. She had fixed her hair and was holding her raincoat. She had lost weight since the funeral, but her flesh still seemed to inhabit her clothes, even when it wasn't there any more. There was a tug around the buttons at her breasts that gave her a wanton look. It was as if Nancy

Reagan had been cast in an am-dram production of a Tennessee Williams play.

Where would you like to go first, Sandy?

I don't know, honey. What do you think? she said. This had been her answer to everything. Today Eithne found it irritating.

We have to wait till dusk to ... Eithne stopped. Redmond O'Neill was fitting a bottle of Black Bush to an optic in the bar off the lobby. She couldn't bear to let him hear the rest of the sentence. *We'll have to wait till dusk to sprinkle the last of Ethan off Malin Head.*

They told Redmond they would be at the table by eight thirty. Outside, it had clouded over. Montbretia and fuchsia combed the hire car as Eithne turned left. They passed through villages erased and written over by the spidery outlines of new towns, unfinished houses that would never be homes, shopping centres without roofs or windows let alone shops. They waited at a pedestrian crossing and watched the green man flash at an empty street.

Where is everybody? asked Sandy.

In a town near the border, they parked behind a closed-down hardware shop. They dipped under overfed hanging baskets and went into a hotel. The foyer smelled of pine disinfectant. Sandy ordered food in the lounge: 'veg' soup tinged acid yellow with synthetic bouillon, a chicken sandwich on thick soft bread that oozed butter and grey stuffing. She said it was delicious; maybe it was. Ethan had said the food in the States was foul, unless you bought at a farmers' market from a hipster with an MBA. But as in every other place, Sandy ate almost nothing. It was as though she hadn't yet realised that what she felt wasn't hunger. It was a ravenous grief.

Eithne excused herself and went outside for a cigarette. The street suddenly filled with the sound of honking horns and a wedding car pulled up, a vintage Rolls-Royce with a V of primrose ribbon pulled taut across the bonnet. The father of the bride got out first, a big man with red hands and a bashful smile. Cars emptied shivering made-up girls and sticky-haired boys on to the street. Eithne went inside and paid the bill. Sandy's face collapsed as the bride beat her way past in stiff skirts. Eithne pretended not to notice.

She took the coast road where she could and found herself naming each bay, each townland.

You know this place so well now, Sandy said.

Now? My father was from here. This is my place, Eithne didn't say.

We won't be able to see the Northern Lights at this time of year, Sandy. Don't you know that? We can wait till dusk if you want, only it won't make any difference.

I guess we could go now.

Eithne doubled back and got on to the road north. Beside her, Sandy became almost animated. She held the handbag to herself and talked about Ethan: how good he had been at sport, and music, and maths (math she called it). How funny he was, and smart, like his father. She talked about him as if he was someone Eithne might like to meet. They went through Malin Village and Sandy murmured approval at its close-cut green and cotton-white shopfronts. They passed a huge church and mouldering bungalows before they reached the blocky fort and modest weather station at Malin Head.

Ethan had booked the trip to Donegal for her birthday. On the way there they walked Derry's walls and ate fat buttery prawns in a restaurant overlooking an abandoned border post. Ethan got up at eight to play golf. To Eithne, it seemed such a grown-up thing to do on a Saturday morning. She lay in the bath for a long time and read a book. In the afternoon they went for a walk on Culdaff Beach and had a pint beside a turf fire in a pub that was showing fake horse races.

Just after four they left for Malin Head. Ethan wanted to see the Northern Lights. When they arrived, there was one other car, a red Toyota with a northern number plate. A couple got out, a trim pair in their sixties in matching blue anoraks. They followed Ethan and Eithne to the information board and stood beside them. According to the forecast, it wouldn't rain until the next afternoon, but Eithne felt sharp, briny spits on her cheeks. She pulled Ethan towards the headland.

Is this far enough north for you? she said. Ethan didn't answer. The other couple were a few feet away. The sky was low and leaden.

We'll see nothing tonight, the man said. They went back to their car.

Jesus. How depressing are they? His 'n' hers Pac a Macs, Eithne said.

This country drives me crazy. Satellite pictures and they still can't give an accurate weather report.

It comes in off the Atlantic. It's unpredictable. She felt defensive, somehow.

Ethan was quiet when they sat down to dinner. He seemed disappointed in that way he had that always seemed churlish to her. It happened when he went to a shop on a Monday and found it closed, or when he couldn't talk someone round to his point of view. She looked up, ready to distract him, make him laugh. He was scowling at the wine list.

Bottle of Merlot, he told the waitress. Murr-low. Not even Murr-low, please.

I'd prefer white. Eithne was surprised at herself, but not as surprised as Ethan.

We always drink red.

Well, I want to drink white tonight. She took the list and pointed at a bottle. Order the red as well. I'm thirsty.

They left the next morning after an early breakfast. On the way home, they stopped at Grianan an Aileach. She got out of the car, leaving Ethan with his camera and guidebook. She went inside the ring fort. She had worried that it would seem small, less majestic than it had when she was young. It still stunned her. She tramped the soft grass and climbed up the stone terraces, too tall now to hug herself to the walls as she walked around them.

Her father had taken them there to see the solstice once. A rod of sunlight had dissected the circular fort, and seemed to cut across Inch Island, across the Foyle and Swilly waters. Even on a day like this, she thought the drab of cloud and field and lough beautiful. When Ethan came into the circle she was standing in the centre, feet apart, as if straddling the line of the sun.

What the hell? said Ethan. He didn't wait for an answer. He told her the history of the fort, facts he had read from the information board and the guidebook, camera slung heavily around his neck. What kind of knowledge was that?

On the drive back to Dublin they didn't talk much. He dropped her at the spinster house before he returned the hire car. He said he would message her later. He didn't. She thought little of it until the next day, when his secretary came to her desk to ask where he was.

The cause of death was a heart attack. Eithne and the caretaker of the building found him lying on his bed clad in black and orange Lycra, still with his trainers on. The caretaker opened the windows – to let his spirit out, he said. While they waited for the ambulance and police she lay on the bed beside him. His hair was frizzy, like Sandy's when she got off the plane. Eithne had never seen it look like that before and wondered how much time he spent making it not frizzy when he was alive. All the things she hadn't known about him.

Later, she sat with the caretaker and looked at footage of him leaving the building. She watched him come out of the lift and bend to pull the tongue straight under the laces of his left shoe. She watched him raise a couple of fingers in salute at the caretaker and take off across the concourse. She watched him pause at the door and bend to breathe, one hour and eight minutes later. But where had he run to?

Eithne's cousin was a Guard. He accessed the city's CCTV footage and traced Ethan's route. Cameras had captured him as he ran along the Liffey, past the Four Courts. The last images were after Blackhall Place. She watched him stand under a lamp post at the bottom of her street and look up towards her house. She watched him turn back.

The company informed his parents. Eithne told them to pass on her phone number and received a call from his father within the hour. Bob came to Dublin the next day to identify his son. He asked Eithne if she wanted to see him but she said no. It was enough to have found him.

There was a small service in Dublin before the body was flown to America. Eithne asked her mother to attend. Ethan's father seemed to expect it.

I never realised they were that serious, her mother told Bob. I only met the poor chap the once.

Bob bought Eithne a ticket to the States. Within a few minutes of landing, she realised why. She had been cast as the tragic young fiancée. Ethan had told his father that he was taking her to Donegal. He planned to propose. But he didn't, and Eithne couldn't say so. They mistook her mortification for a broken heart.

She found herself paired with Sandy in the funeral car, at the service, at lunch. Bob's second wife had arranged everything: the flowers, music, readings. Bob wrote the eulogy; he talked for twenty minutes and didn't mention Sandy. Eithne felt sorry for her yet found her pathetic. She had let Diane replace her as wife, almost as mother too. After the cremation his parents split his ashes. Ethan would have been amazed; they managed it without the services of a lawyer. Sandy contacted Eithne a few weeks later and asked her to accompany her on a trip around Ireland to scatter his remains. She had only met Ethan thirteen months earlier, and he had been dead for four of them. But what could she say?

On a clear day you can see Tory Island from Malin Head, a stubborn hump in the water. Today there was a dull white sky. Eithne helped Sandy across the basalt terrace towards the water's edge. The sea came over the rocks with gentle slaps as Sandy opened the handbag for the last time.

There is so little of him left, Sandy said. Eithne watched her put her hand inside the urn and pull out one of the little plastic bags she had divided him into for convenience. Eithne pictured her at her kitchen counter, spooning her powdered son into sachets as though he was a street drug she was getting ready for sale. Eithne wondered which part it was. A hand. A lung. A ventricle from the heart that had given out in February.

What did Bob do with his share? she asked.

He and Diane brought him to all the big places he had visited back home. The Empire State, places like that. Augusta, though he never got to play there.

And you just wanted to bring him to Ireland?

Oh no, honey. I brought him to Spring Valley Drive, where we used to live.

His father had gone on a tour of America with his second wife. Sandy had taken Ethan back to the house they lived in when he was a child, before the divorce. Two families had lived there since they left. The woman of the house asked Sandy in for iced tea when she saw her crying outside. She let her look around the garden and brought her upstairs. Ethan's old bedroom was a little girl's bedroom. Nothing remained of him. She knew this would be the case, but found it devastating. She stood on the street outside the house, patting her pocket, trying to think of the right place. He was everywhere, and nowhere. In the end, she walked around the block and sprinkled him along the grass verges where he had thrown his bike.

Sandy tapped the last sachet against the back of her hand, like the boy in Barack Obama Plaza had with the sugar.

We came up here to see the Northern Lights. It was cloudy. I think he was disappointed, said Eithne.

Poor Ethan. He never really learned that you can't always get what you want.

Sandy turned her back to the wind. She seasoned the Atlantic breeze with the last of her son, her face bright with relief, with gratitude that she hadn't been left to do it alone. There was a smudge in a corner of the sachet. Sandy held it out and Eithne took it from her. She tucked the last of Ethan into the pocket of her jeans. She might come back in the winter, on a clear night.

HANDS

He left his mother at the edge of the well and climbed the stone steps to the grotto. There were trinkets on all the trees, flashes of colour that rattled as he passed, but the holly tree was heavy with them. The branches were strung with dozens of weathered charms. Cloudy glass rosary beads and miraculous medals, floral ribbon tied in limp bows. A Padre Pio picture in a leather frame, a tiny Rubik Cube swinging against it. There were scraps of gingham cloth, a glittery scrunchie, a paisley neck-tie. A gust of wind came through the glade, and the tree chinkled with the desperate tat that hung from it. Jason went back down the steps to Margie, his mother. The Bag for Life was full.

Are you right? he said. She reached a hand up and he hauled her to her feet.

By the time he had driven a hundred yards up the road, the scent was so strong he had to open the car windows.

Don't start, she said. Unless you have a better idea for getting money.

I'm not starting, he said. I'm saying nothing.

When they got back to the house Margie made tea and got out her sewing things. She spread a piece of muslin on the kitchen table and cut it into four rectangles.

You said there was only one coming, he said.

I got a text this morning. You may as well do another while you're at it, she said.

Jason didn't believe her. There were three or four coming every week, always on a Wednesday, the day Stacey had agreed to let him see the child. Margie tipped the straggles of wilting greenery on to the table. Wood anemones, bluebells, wild garlic. She tied them into tight bundles and folded the cloth around them. She stitched the sides and laid out each pouch as it was finished, tossing the last across the table at him. As he caught it, the doorbell rang.

How's that for timing, she said and went out to the hallway. When she had settled the caller in the sitting room she came back into the kitchen with a box of biscuits and an envelope.

Who is it?

Tommy Dunne, his name is. From out Ballisodare way.

What's wrong with him?

The throat.

Fuck's sake, said Jason. The throats were the worst of all. He went into the sitting room.

The man was by the fireside. The TV remote control was still on the arm of the chair from the previous night, and he was looking at it with complete concentration. The very sick ones often did that, found something to fixate on. Most of them came reluctantly, pestered into it by wives and daughters unable to accept a bad prognosis. Tommy Dunne looked wretched. His head was hairless except for a wisp above his left ear. There was a plump steroid glow about his jowls and cheeks, the rest of his body skeletal.

Jason pulled a chair close to him and took his hands in his. He could feel the fabric of the plasters the man had stuck on his chemo-rotten fingernails and was grateful. Sometimes they bared themselves to his hands, offered raw scars and wounds that were scarcely closed, believing his cure would better pass into them unencumbered by dressings and bandages. The man closed his eyes and lowered his head. Margie passed Jason a muslin bag. It was warmish, the flowers and herbs beginning their putrefaction. He pressed it to the bandage at the man's throat, heard a faint whistle from the drain in his voice box. Jason put his other hand on his sternum, felt the rise and fall of his breath, the gurgle of phlegm and tar. The man put his hand over Jason's and held it there, at his heart, and Jason felt it. Not a charge of energy coursing out through his own fingers, like Margie said, the mystical powers of a seventh son. It was coming from Tommy Dunne. A swell of faith, of want.

Jason helped him up. Tommy Dunne made slow progress through the hall, pausing to steady himself on the bamboo table, the papered wall. He turned to Jason at the door and put a finger on his bandage. Thanks, son, he quacked. Jason watched a woman arrange him gently in the passenger seat of a Nissan Micra. Tommy held a hand up as she drove off.

Jason went into the kitchen. Margie was at the table, opening the box of biscuits. She bit a chocolate chip cookie and took the money out of the envelope. She gave two twenties to Jason and put one in her purse.

Is that your booking fee? he said.

I'm doing my best, she said. Make sure and give that to the Rainey one.

That man has cancer. I can't cure cancer. And stop calling her the Rainey one.

He didn't expect you to cure the cancer. He just wants relief.

It's not right charging them.

I don't charge them.

Well, how come they always leave an even sixty euro?

Bring me the laundry basket from the landing and stop annoying my shite.

Unreal, he said and went upstairs. He sat on his bed and sent Stacey Rainey a message. *I have a few bob for you. I'll be there shortly.* She read it and didn't reply. He lifted clothes off his bedroom floor and brought the dirty laundry down to the kitchen.

The next one will be handy enough, said Margie, into the drum of the washing machine.

The girl was about four. Her grandmother was in her forties, peroxide-blonde with sparkly purple eyeshadow. She has herself destroyed, she said, pulling the child's sleeve up. Her skinny arms were spotted with round red sores, the crusty scabs rubbed away by her fingers. Jason let her sit on her granny's knee and placed a bag over the crop of spots on her inner arm.

Close your eyes and count to ten, he said. She did as he told her, eyelids twitching. Open them.

She looked down. They're still there, she said and started to cry.

It'll take a few days, said Margie, opening a tin of lollipops. The child chose one with a pink wrapper. She tore it open and a drip of snot fell on to her hand as she put it in her mouth.

The granny picked up a framed newspaper photograph of Jason in a Bob the Builder jumper, an elderly woman bent in front of him, under the headline THE BOY WITH THE HANDS. I remember you at that age, she said. You sorted our Josie out when she had chicken pox.

He has a gift, said Margie and saw them out.

Jason didn't know what it was that he did but had figured early that what was required of him was concentration. He learned to close his eyes as he put his hands on them. He said rhymes in his head and sang little songs. His favourite was the one he had heard on the school bus that didn't make sense but had a sing-song tune:

My granny went to Scotland,
she nearly scored a goal,
she caught her tits and done the splits
and shoved it up her hole.

He'd sing it ten times and then open his eyes. He's praying, they would whisper. The wee size of him, and he's praying. He didn't know if he had a gift or not. They came and he laid his hands on them. Once or twice there had been a problem. A hurler with a sprain demanded a refund when he was declared unfit for a county final. Someone else rang a local radio show and called him a con artist. Margie responded by bringing him to a lab in Galway to have thermal images taken. They showed red pools of heat where Jason touched them. She went on the radio to clear his name, and the sick people were still coming.

He washed his hands at the kitchen sink, in water so hot he could hardly stand it. Margie marched in and turned the tap off. You're scalded, she said.

I'm going to Stacey's. I can't have this shit on my hands.

You never catch anything off them.

He has a gift. Is that it? What if Cian catches something?

He won't. When are you off?

Now. Have you the rest of that money?

The doorbell rang. You'll have to wait half an hour.

How many more?

This is the last. I swear.

Windburn McGlinchey was wearing Grinch pyjama bottoms and a shirt and tie. I'm killed with the itch, he said. He dropped into the armchair and sat with his hands hovering at his knee, as if he wanted to rip the leg from his body. Margie carried over a stool and carefully hoisted the diseased limb on to it.

Now, she said.

You're a lady, he said with dignity. He pulled his trouser leg up, revealing an expanse of calf the same shade of puce as his face. Margie peeled away the dressing and regarded the ulcer with grim compulsion, the way one might a road accident. Jason beckoned her out to the kitchen.

Cover it up.

He wants you to touch it.

I am not putting one of those manky pouches on that wound. He'll get gangrene.

Ah, come on.

Cover it or I'm not going near him. There's a smell off it.

When the dressing was back on, Jason sat beside Windburn. He held the bag to the leg and closed his eyes. After he thought five minutes had passed, he patted Windburn's arm and went upstairs. He didn't come out until he heard the front door close.

Margie roared up the stairs at him. What are you playing at? If word gets out that you're not arsed it'll be bad …

He came out of his room. Bad for business? he said. You might as well say it.

She slapped €120 on the bamboo table. Call it what you like, she said. You do your thing and they pay. But you need to make an effort. Fair is fair.

Margie went into the kitchen and banged the door. Jason ran down the stairs and put his jacket on. He took the cash and left the house.

The evening traffic was getting heavy, a stream of cars coming towards him, headed for the villages their drivers had moved to during the boom that they now couldn't afford to leave. Stacey hadn't replied to his message. He'd just turn up; she wouldn't make a scene in front of Cian. Maybe he should buy him a present; he had enough cash. The two units that fronted the shopping centre were vacant again, their windows covered with paper. Boys and girls in school uniforms stood in leery huddles outside it, shouting over at each other. He went through the wide glass doors. Around him, women pushing buggies hung with shopping bags zigzagged across the concourse. What was he doing? Absent fathers brought presents. He wasn't like that. The only time they'd met, his own father had given him a bucket of Meccano. It had already been opened and Jason was Cian's age, too young to figure out how to use it. Margie had put a spanner in his hand and followed the man to the kitchen, leaving Jason in front of a scatter of wheels and nuts and bolts, listening to the rise of his mother's voice, the man's strange accent. He didn't remember his father leaving, but he'd never forget when his mother did, a few days later. He turned and went back on to the street.

McGuinness's door was open. Jason hovered in the porch. The dense knot of fairy lights above the bar seemed to be winking at him. He took in a lungful of stale hops and started walking again, turning right at the bridge. The river was low, pattering over the weir. A life-buoy was caught on the branch of a sally tree, tipping into the water. Where the river widened into the lake, the path split in two: one a rough trail along the bank, lined with elder and dogwood; the other a strip of tarmac that led to the turn for Stacey's place. He went on the footpath and crossed the road. The houses in her estate were built around a grassy circle, a megalithic burial site. The church had added a white crucifix and several statues that were bent in various states of devotion among the ancient stones. There were small bikes and scooters strewn in some of the gardens. Stacey's lawn was tufty, uncut since the previous autumn.

He stood on the doorstep and rang the bell. She didn't answer. He went to the window. Cian was on the couch. Jason knocked on the glass and Cian waved at him and slid on to the floor.

Stacey opened the front door and put her head around the frame.

It's not a good time, she said. She had on an orange chenille jumper that leached the colour from her face.

Look, I'm here now.

I told him you were coming for lunch.

What did you do that for?

Because you said you'd be here, Jason. He sat at the table until half two, waiting for you.

Shit.

You need to go. I'm about to do his physio.

Let me help you.

She was closing the door against him when Cian came into the hall. He ducked under Stacey's elbow and reached his arms up at his father.

Hey, wee man, Jason said, picking him up. Cian landed a salty kiss on his lips. Stacey had gone inside. Jason followed her.

Wash your hands, she said, as if she was telling him for the third or fourth time. He put Cian on the couch and went to the kitchen. Bottles of hand sanitiser and

Milton and liquid soap were lined near the sink, packets of wipes and tissues on the windowsill. He washed his hands and shook them dry.

Stacey had taken the cushions off the couch and was laying sheets of newspaper on the carpet. There was a plastic crate of medication and nebulisers on the coffee table, a set of Mr Men books stacked beside it. Jason sat down and lifted Cian on to his lap. He placed a hand on his chest, the other on his back. When Stacey spoke, her voice was calm.

Big breath in. Daddy will count.

Each breath took tremendous effort, but for all the gasping, and the huffing and puffing, Cian seemed to be taking in little air. Stacey laid him on his side across Jason's knee, his head hanging lower than his body. She cupped her hand and began to clap his chest. The sound was dreadful, the thud of the hand against flat bone, the dull echo in the silted chambers. After what seemed like an age Cian began to retch, shoulders heaving. He vomited on to the newspaper. When he was finished his face was blotched purple and his eyes were streaming. Jason put his hands around him again, shoring him up. When his breath had settled into its quick, shallow rhythm he slid off Jason's knee and reached for the remote control. Stacey wrapped the sick as if it was a fish supper and brought it to the kitchen.

Jason went to lift Cian, but the child winced at the pressure of the hands on his ribcage, so he let him go. What are you watching? he said.

Cartoons.

Jason took a jigsaw puzzle from a stack by the toybox. On the lid there was a picture of ruddy boys in red jerseys playing football. We'll do something else for a change, he said. He cleared a space on the table, laid out the pieces and patted the floor. Cian knelt on the carpet. He put the corners in place and finished it in under a minute. He had scarcely looked away from the television. Jason should have brought him something new. His world was so small: this cluttered room, his stuffy bedroom.

He went into the kitchen. Stacey was folding laundry. Her hands were shiny, an older woman's hands. You're great with him, Jason said.

There's fuck all coming up. Since he got that cold I'm having to do it three or four times a day. His wee chest is bruised.

What does the doctor say?

What can she say? Go in and sit with him, will you? I want to get ahead of myself.

He woke on the couch with Stacey standing over him. Cian hadn't moved. Was I asleep long? he said.

About half an hour.

Sorry. You should have woken me up. He got his jacket from the kitchen. He took the bundle of money from the inside pocket and handed it to her. It reeked of garlic; a poultice of banknotes. He shook the jacket out as if he was going to put it on. Then he paused as if he'd just had an idea. We could order a takeaway, he said. If you fancy a night off cooking.

Stacey tucked the cash in her back pocket. Grand, she said, without looking at him. I'll feed Cian first.

Jason told the boy he could eat in front of the television. Stacey ordered them both to the table. She had prepared trees of broccoli and coins of carrot, chicken breast and brown pasta. She put the plate in front of Cian and went upstairs. He ate slowly, stopping sometimes to cough. When he was finished, Jason brought him up to the bathroom. The tub was full of bubbles and there was a Disney towel warming on the radiator. Jason loaded Cian's water pistol and let him squirt it at the walls and floor. He shampooed his hair but didn't get all the suds out, so Stacey had to come in and rinse it. She had swapped the horrid jumper for a black top and put on dark eye make-up. They brought him into his room and did the physio again. He kept his dinner down. Jason asked him to choose a bedtime story and had to read the *ABC of Tractors* three times. Stacey turned on the monitor. She bent to tuck Cian in, and there was something so snug in the fit of them that Jason thought for a mad second he might cry.

She had tidied the sitting room. The harsh ceiling light was off, and there were tea lights burning in coloured glass pots along the mantelpiece. The coffee table had been cleared, the paraphernalia of Cian's illness consigned to the corner with the toys and puzzles. Wine and beer and a tray loaded with plates, glasses and cutlery were in their place. Stacey sat in Cian's spot with her feet tucked under herself and, when Jason passed her a drink, she stretched like a cat.

What'll I order? he said.

The usual. She was looking at him, almost smiling. He scrolled through the menu on his phone, hoping it would trigger something, but couldn't remember what they used to order. He asked for his favourites and took a guess on hers. When he reached to refill her glass, her mouth was turned down at the corners. He had got it wrong.

It was after nine when the food came. They were both so hungry its arrival seemed to mitigate her disappointment. He began to load her plate with food, but a rasp sputtered from the monitor and she ran upstairs. The spasm went on for a couple of minutes, the awful percussion of Stacey's hand on Cian's chest beating dully in the speaker. When she came down a thread of mucous was glistening on her top.

Their food had cooled. It looked gelatinous and unnatural. He brought it to the kitchen to reheat it. While the plastic boxes rotated in the microwave, he looked around. The mugs on the stand were china with pastel polka dots. The kitchen cloth was soaking in a small basin of Milton. White wooden letters lined along the windowsill spelled HOME. Just by standing there, he was making the place untidy.

He put on some music, a dreary drum and bass track that made her stiffen with irritation. He turned it off. She put on a film, a romantic comedy where a plain girl who turns out to be a stunner gets a rich man who turns out to be a bollocks, then ends up with his quiet friend. Stacey laughed throughout and, when it was over, reached for the empty wine bottle. Did I drink all that? she said.

Jason yawned and stretched his arms over his head. I'd better get moving, he said. He went to the window and tweaked the blind.

She tipped a pork rib into a plastic tub and spoke without looking up. You can stay, she said, the previous exchange a farce that played out sometimes.

She brought the monitor upstairs to her room. The spotlights that were trained on the statues and stones outside cast a cold bluish light over the gingham duvet cover, the bottles and jars on her dressing table. The air was warm and faintly perfumed. He bent to untie his laces and, when he straightened up, she had stripped to her knickers. She shuddered and got under the covers. He took his clothes off and got in beside her. She rolled on top of him and he put his hands on her hips. The Boy with the Hands, my arse, she said. They're fucking freezing.

Afterwards she fell asleep with her face nestled in his armpit. The lights on the monitor winked erratically, faltering, quickening, mimicking the sounds from Cian's chest. Sometimes it flashed with a sharp cough and Stacey held her breath until she heard Cian's. Jason thought about the nights he'd spent in the spare room at his granny's house when Margie disappeared. Lying awake in the dark, spooked by the red light from the Sacred Heart picture on the landing. He never asked where she had gone, or whether she was coming back; maybe he was afraid to hear the answer. One day she came into the kitchen and fell to her knees in front of him. Her bracelets dug into him as she held him, and when she spoke her voice was slow and quiet. You are a very special boy, she said, and I'll never leave you again. The sick people had started coming after that.

They came because Margie said he was the seventh son of a seventh son. Stacey was the only person who had openly questioned it, swinging around with one of the framed newspaper articles in her hand, declaring *You're an only child!* He told her the story Margie had told him, about the weeks she spent wandering the streets of Strabane looking for his father, a rangy, maudlin Chuck Berry fan she had met at a festival. She found him by the trolley bay outside Crazy Prices, surrounded by a fat woman and six skinny male children. Stacey had asked Jason if he believed her. He said he didn't know. She asked if he believed he could heal the sick and the answer had come so easily: I can make them feel better.

The coughing began after dawn. Stacey woke at once and crawled to the end of the bed, her arse sticking up at him. What are you looking for? he asked.

She held up a pair of black knickers, the waistband rolled around itself. Go in to him! she said and pulled them on under the covers.

Cian was flushed. His lips were red and cracked and his chest sounded like a coffee percolator. Jason put him on his front and cupped his hand. He willed it to come down on the small back, but he didn't know what to do. He turned him over and laid his hands on him, the way he had with Tommy Dunne, Windburn McGlinchey, and the little girl who chose the pink lollipop. He closed his eyes. He recited the rhyme. He said a prayer. He felt no heat, no surge of hope or desperation. Just the quick, arrhythmic beat of Cian's heart.

ONCE UPON A PAIR
OF WHEELS

He was loading his tools into the van at the end of his first day when she realised it was him. She was scarcely out of the car, heels skittling the gravel, when she spoke.

Jesus Christ, she said.

The child was strapped into an oversized booster in the back seat, huge and pale like his father. Niamh knocked the window and he got out, dragging a sombre grey satchel. She ushered him up the steps and unlocked the front door, swinging it open in front of him. Go and change out of your uniform, Roo, she said. I'll just be a sec.

What are the odds? said Aidan.

What are you doing here?

My mate Robbie got the contract for the groundwork. I do all the landscaping for him.

Landscaping?

Aidan spread his hands, an involuntary gesture that must have looked rueful. What do you do? he asked.

Law, she said, for my sins.

That's great.

How long will you be here? she said, frowning at the rubble around the new driveway, the overturned ground.

A week or so if the weather holds out.

The boy was still in the doorway, swinging the door back and forward. I'll get your *goûter* in a sec, Roo, she called. It's French, she added apologetically, an afternoon snack. We have a place in the Languedoc.

Nice. How old is your son?

He'll be eight in a couple of days.

Eight, said Aidan. The same age as the boy he had knocked down and killed.

Look, I'd better go in, said Niamh. We'll talk properly one of the days. She turned and went inside.

He pulled the door across the side of the van and got into the driver's seat, reversing slowly away from the house. The boy was kneeling on the living-room windowsill. He took a bite from the piece of food he held in his left hand and raised it at Aidan in farewell. Niamh was standing behind him with her arms folded.

Aidan turned out of her street and on to the main road. It was a cold evening, but dry, and the traffic was light. People in suits and school uniforms were walking purposefully along the pavements, as though someone was waiting for them. He lived less than a mile away, on a tree-lined avenue of large Victorian red-bricks in their own grounds, in the only house that was still divided into flats. He drove through the stone gateposts and got out to open the rotting double doors on the garage. The grow lamp had been on all day. He grew specimen plants from seed. Lupins and delphiniums and a variety of cannabis called Blue Dream that had been engineered to minimise paranoia. Their leaves were similar, and in the unlikely event anyone ever found them his landlady would be able to plead ignorance. Mrs Ferguson claimed to have Parkinson's disease and sometimes knocked his door for a 'medicinal' smoke. He had seen little evidence of the condition on her, aside from a faint tremor of the hands he suspected was caused by the Mateus Rosé she bought by the case. Aidan's diagnosis was that she was lonely and liked being stoned. They had a lot in common. He parked the van in the garage and locked the doors behind him.

The house was elegantly dilapidated. The Anaglypta paper in the hall was the colour of tobacco, and there were dents in the dado rail from bicycle handlebars. His flat had once been the drawing room. It was warmed by inefficient storage heaters but had a grand mahogany fireplace that he used most nights. Mrs Ferguson had let him paint the floorboards black. There was a wing-backed leather chair and footstool with rosewood legs to the left of the fireplace, a brass bed with a thick, saggy mattress to its right. Women fell heavily for it all. The flat and his vinyl collection and the line he had perfected in arcane self-deprecation. Most didn't mind that he had been to prison. One or two had actively liked it, like Sadhbh, the bookseller, who sent her own poetry to men on Death Row and on their first night seemed rather disappointed that he didn't savage her and spit her cheek across the room.

He put a frozen cottage pie in the microwave oven. When it was hot, he slid it on to a plate and brought it to the table. He opened his laptop and typed *Niamh Cosgrove solicitor*. He liked to click down through the links in the order in which they appeared. The only social media she did was on a business networking site. Her CV was impressive, each position leading to something better, a fast and steady trajectory. She was senior partner in a firm that specialised in employment law. He was heartened that this was the field she had chosen. His own ambitions had once been similarly civic-minded. He had wanted to be an architect who designed grand public buildings. Maybe that was why she had appeared so disappointed to see him swinging a shovel into the back of a van. Sucking in her bottom lip as though he was less than he should be.

He opened the magazine feature on her wedding again. She had met Clive in a corporate box at Lansdowne. He was a management consultant, based in London but looking forward to the commute to their new home in Dublin. He had a shiny pate that may once have been ginger and one of those loose, rugby-smashed faces that made the woman beside him look especially pretty.

He rolled a joint and put on a record. He had given his television to Mrs Ferguson after he had gone missing from a job for two days. Robbie found him in bed with an empty Bushmills bottle watching *Cash in the Attic*. You'd want to knock this shit on the head, Robbie had said. He meant Aidan should stop drinking altogether but he had only managed to give up whiskey and daytime television.

He got out the plan for Niamh's garden. Robbie had scribbled it on a page from a jotter. It was the sort of scheme most people chose. Californian lilac and rosemary, mallow and lavender. A dwarf cherry blossom with an underplanting of black tulips. A garden you could neglect. It was so predictable it offended him. Niamh's house had been renovated with care. It still had the original windows, with angular panes and pastel-coloured stained glass. When they were students she listened to Lottie Lenya and bought discounted books about Eileen Gray. It made him feel like he still knew her to see she had found an art deco house to live in. He took down the book with the photograph of a garden planted in the 1930s. Pale grasses against a curved white wall. Rubbery-limbed palms and feathery Japanese maples. He began to draw.

He went to bed at eleven. His phone throbbed with a message from Alice. She was speaking at a conference in San Sebastián about taboos and the female body. They had met when he was working in a public park. She had been commissioned to make something on the theme of fertility. When the six-foot wooden figure based on a Sheela-na-gig was unveiled, broad features set in an expression of stupefied lust, fat hands revealing a deep dimple of a vagina, there was uproar. He knew from the hour she was drunk and looking for phone sex. These long-distance intimacies made him cringe but were preferable to having her around. She had begun to leave things behind when she stayed over. A tube of moisturiser, a book, a scarf. He put his phone on silent.

When he woke in the morning he felt hollowed out. He'd had the dream again. Sometimes the recollection was complete, but this morning he only remembered the moment of impact. A sudden loom, a dimming. Surprise widening out from the boy's eyes. The blood and cartilage of the small nose spreading across the glass. Was this how Niamh's day was beginning?

He brewed a pot of espresso and brought it to the table. He studied the drawings again. They needed more information: accurate measurements and an idea of how the sun moved across the garden through the day.

Her driveway was empty. He put on a pair of gloves that were shiny with compressed soil. He opened out a BabySkip bag and began to fill it with clumps of dried cement, jagged grey stones. Robbie complained that he took too long over this, that he was too particular. It seemed to Aidan it was the most important thing, to bed the plants down into clean, warm soil. Robbie said that was the stoner coming out in him.

He had been working for over an hour when the front door opened. A very thin girl with white-blonde hair pulled tightly off her face handed him a key. Niamh says you can use kitchen, she said, but not in your boots. She went back inside.

He took a break at eleven. The girl was at the sink, polishing a copper saucepan that looked like it had never been used. He stepped out of his boots. There was a hole in the toe of one of his socks. The nail was crumbly and yellow. She stared at it, then showed him the toilet and the cupboard where the tea and coffee were kept. He made tea and stood on the doormat to drink it. The kitchen had wooden cupboards painted a watery blue, the original cream tiles covering the wall behind the old Aga. There were clothes draped over a pulley above it, a scent of washing powder. The girl took her gloves off from time to time to reverse the boy's vests and pants that were drying there.

Have you worked here long? he said.

Four months. My friend was here before but didn't like it.

Do you like it?

It's money.

He rinsed his cup and left it on the rack. I'm Aidan, by the way, he said.

She nodded. He went back outside.

At one, he walked to a cafe. He sat at a table by the window and ordered soup. He liked this place. It was where he had found Niamh again the previous summer, sitting just a few inches from him. So close he could smell the spice in her chai latte, hear her phone buzz against the pine tabletop. She only lived a couple of streets away. He had sat in the van and watched her walk around her house with the foreman, voguing at the roof with her hands, maybe trying to picture where the Velux windows would be. Such luck that the house was a building site. He persuaded Robbie to tender for the groundwork, and here he was.

He rested between slurps to look around. The room was full of women. Older women with beige hair drinking milky coffee and stabbing at tartlets with pastry forks. Younger women with thatches of bleeding beetroot and rocket in front of them. He wiped his sleeve across the window. On the kerb outside, more women pulled up in solid, shiny cars and left minutes later with paint cards and swatches of fabric, paper wraps of organic meat and bunches of leafy vegetables. Deliberate selections made casual by the slam of car doors and quick steps across the pavement.

In the afternoon he worked fast. The soil was rich but light, a goldish loam that hadn't clogged, even after months of rain and hail. You could grow almost anything here. He cut a line into the ground with the spade, making room in his mind for a giant cardoon. A tall architectural plant that would work beside delphiniums and hybrid thistles. Maybe a bronze euphorbia.

He went inside to use the toilet. There was a smell of sweet winey meat coming from the Aga. The girl was gone. She hadn't told him her name and he didn't like that he now thought of her as 'the cleaner'. He left his boots at the door and crossed the kitchen. The small bathroom had beige marble tiles and a watercolour of a rainy beach. He came out and paused to look at the fridge door. There was a reminder card for a dental check-up, a timetable for junior orchestra attached by a Save the Date fridge magnet for a wedding in Scotland in September. A photograph of the house in France. It was old, red-roofed. The door and shutters were painted olive green and red geraniums were trailing from window boxes down the stone facade.

Outside he went at the bed with a spade. Turning the ground over, each twist unearthing something. A chip of brick. A piece of coloured glass. He stayed at it until dusk, hoping she would swing into the drive again. It was almost six when he got into his van. Lights came on in the house as the first Angelus bell rang out on the radio.

The sitting room filling with a look of quiet comfort on the final stroke.

He showered when he got home and cooked dinner in his underwear. Spaghetti carbonara that hadn't evolved much from his student days, made with a sachet of Colman's cheese sauce and rasher bits. Niamh used to throw in a handful of peas, *so we don't die*. He brought his plate to the table and listened to the sounds from the flat upstairs. The stagger of a toddler's feet across the boards. The scrape of a dining chair.

He made notes on the plan he had drawn for the garden. Erased the pampas grass and sketched in a giant cardoon. He drew and rubbed, moving the plants around the page until he could see height and depth in the arrangement. He had developed a talent for visualising how a space would look after five years, ten, twenty. The ability surprised him. He'd had an utter lack of foresight when he was young. When it shouldn't have mattered, but it had.

He sat in the chair and rolled a spliff. His phone rang. It was Robbie. How's the job going? he said.

Grand.

Have you met the wife?

Yeah.

She's a cunt. Nice, though. The boys were perving on her all week.

I was thinking of altering the plans. Planting stuff that would work better with the house.

Give her what she asked for.

Robbie had heard all about Niamh. In prison he had watched Aidan wait for a phone call, a letter, a visit. Later, he had watched him drink himself into fights, out of jobs, out of relationships. Move on, man, he had been telling him for years. Move on. If he found out Aidan was working on Niamh's garden, he would pull him out of it.

OK, Aidan said. I'll leave it. He and Niamh had a shared geography. They walked the same streets, used the same shops. He didn't want to fuck it up. Granted, he had taken risks. Parked on her road, sitting in the van outside her house, smoking until his tongue was creamy. There was no need for any of that now. He was in.

His phone went again an hour later. Alice was coming back the next day and she literally couldn't wait to see him. She sent him a photograph of a pair of tits he was fairly sure weren't hers. He got into bed and phoned her back. She sounded sexy, if faintly comical, murmuring obscenities in a Mayo accent. He came in a T-shirt and lay awake for a long time. When he finally slept it was fitful and left him feeling worse than the previous morning. The dream had been sequential, yet grainy, darkly-lit. The small heap of broken bones, so far from the car. Niamh vomiting in a lay-by a mile up the road while he sat, hands still gripping the steering wheel, staring at the rusty smear on the window.

He bought a sausage roll in a petrol station on the way to her house. Her car was in the driveway. She appeared with the child as he was lifting the tools out. Her hair was held off her face with a silver clip and her grey suit was sharply cut, almost tight.

Roo is eight today, she said.

Happy birthday, man, said Aidan.

We're going for pizza tonight, said Roo.

Nice one, said Aidan.

Roo gave him a small smile and climbed into the back seat.

How are you getting on? said Niamh.

Grand, he said. I've almost finished preparing the ground.

She was looking at him keenly, as if she had never heard anything like it. It's weird having you here. Doing this, she said, waving her hand vaguely at the garden.

What do you want me to do? he said.

Finish it, obviously. But we should talk.

He managed to stop the digging and hoeing by lunchtime and went inside to make tea. There was an iron plugged in and gasping on a board, the sound of clothes tumbling in a drier. He brought the mug outside and sat in the van to drink it and eat the sausage roll. Alice sent him a message. She had just boarded her plane and would pass his house on the Aircoach at seven. Should she call in? Sure, he replied. He spent the afternoon working on the rockery along the other side of the driveway, trailing the old plants out, the gnarled houseleeks and bedraggled dianthus. He left before five.

The flat smelled fusty. He pulled up the sash window and sat on the sill to smoke. He went to the kitchen and washed the pot and bowl and fork from the previous night. There was a creel of ash logs by the hearth. He took the best ones and made a fire. He walked around to the wine shop. It was doing 3 for 2 on a young Rioja. He bought some cheese, a tin of pâté and oatcakes as well. Niamh's car was outside the cafe. He glimpsed her at a table to the side. She was sitting opposite Roo with her laptop open. The boy was scooping ice cream from a glass sundae dish.

Alice was on the doorstep with her bags when he got home. She had the slightly defensive air she often had in the first few minutes of their meeting, but mellowed when she saw that he had gone to some trouble. He put on music she liked that he didn't. They sat at the table and she cut pieces from the cheese and passed them to him. She looked at Niamh's plans, told him he was wasted on domestic jobs. When they went to bed she pushed her arse into his groin and put her head on the bend of his elbow. He left her there until his arm was asleep and her breath was coming in tiny sighs. He rolled away from her. He thought about Niamh and her son in the cafe and couldn't remember what he had hoped to see when he drove over there.

Early in the morning Alice turned to him shyly, as if the dirty words of a couple of nights ago had been spoken by other people. When they got up she washed her face and tied up her hair. The skin around her eyes was puckered with dehydration from the wine and the flight. She looked both fresh-faced and tired. Her cabin bag was open on the floor. As she was closing it he pointed at the tallboy.

Don't forget your stuff, he said.

She stood still for a moment and blinked once, slowly. She threw her things into the bag and zipped it up. I'm too old for this shit, she said. The door banged behind her.

When he got to Niamh's house her car was gone. The cleaner came up the driveway as he was getting out of the van.

Hey, he said.

Hi.

How many days a week are you here?

Three, but tonight she is going out so I babysit.

He spent the morning cutting lengths of plastic sheeting and tucking them tightly over the prepared earth, laying the strips side by side until no soil was visible, boring holes for the shrubs and flowers.

At one he went into the kitchen. The cleaner was gone. There was a birthday cake on the counter with a note on it: *Help yourself.* It had hardly been touched. Aidan cut himself a big slice. It was a chocolate sponge iced in ganache, too rich for a child. Not that poor Roo was like a child, with his sober satchel and his after-school *goûter*.

He went down the hall to the bedrooms. The boy's room was part of the original house: cosy, with navy-blue curtains and a long floating shelf of Enid Blyton books. Next door was a guest room with a queen-sized bed dressed in white and a basket of miniature toiletries on one of the nightstands. The extension was at the end of the corridor. He pushed the door open. One wall and part of the ceiling were glass, and even on a winter's day like this the room was warm and bright. He went into the walk-in wardrobe. Clive's suits were hanging in polythene sheaths, and there was a stack of jumpers in girly colours that only a seventeen-stone former prop could get away with. Niamh's clothes were slightly untidy and, when he buried his face in them, gave up the scent of gardenia.

By the time Niamh pulled up in her car the beds were ready for planting. She let Roo in and told him to take a small piece of cake.

Does eight o'clock work for you? she asked Aidan.

Tonight? Yeah. Grand.

When he got home his flat smelled ripe, an odour like feet coming from the shrunken pieces of cheese rind.

The glasses and empty wine bottle were still on the table. His pillows were smudged with mascara and the spunky T-shirt was lying on the floor. He showered and changed. He sat in the chair and rolled a joint. Niamh had arranged a babysitter without asking if he was free. Presumed he had nothing better to do. He wouldn't tidy up. The mess made it look almost as though he had a life. He smoked the joint as he walked to the pub.

The place they agreed on wasn't far from where they lived, but a world away from Niamh's road. It was one of those suburban pubs that had replaced a genuine Victorian bar with a fake one from a catalogue. He had suggested a place in town, but she said he'd take too much explaining. The statement was open to interpretation, and he had found it hard to let it go. They ordered at the counter. She asked for white wine. After the barman lined up a selection of quarter-bottles she ordered a gin and tonic. They sat in a pine snug. There was a football match on the television and the barman delivered a basket of cocktail sausages and chips with their drinks.

Aidan hadn't eaten anything but cake all day and devoured it.

Was it awful? she said suddenly.

It was tasty enough. Greasy, though.

You know what I mean. Prison, obviously.

Do you mean was I gang-raped by bodybuilders from Finglas every night?

Christ, she said.

Well, I wasn't. But it wasn't the best year of my life, he said.

It wasn't the worst, either. A prison officer had felt sorry for him and brought him to help in the garden. Robbie was working there already, at the end of a sentence for possession with intent to supply. They had grown grotesquely large marrows and heirloom tomatoes and dwarf cannabis plants they said were Asian salad leaves, and the sentence had passed quickly. The years after were harder, when he had to go home and endure his parents' attempts at forgiving him.

I drew up a new plan for your garden. There are some cool plants on it that might really work with your house.

She didn't say anything. They ordered another drink and she told him about people they had known in college. They all seemed to have lives like hers. I looked your firm up, he said. Employment law. Fighting the man.

That's not what we do. My clients are companies, employers. We defend constructive dismissal claims, get around the legislation. Finding ways through the grey areas, that's what we're good at.

She asked about his mother.

She's dead nine years, he said. He didn't tell her the cause was cancer of the heart. It would have sounded too melodramatic.

She asked if he was with someone and he made the thing with Alice sound more than it was. She glanced at her watch and he pretended to yawn. He suggested they walk down the road and try to hail a taxi. When they were near his house he offered her a nightcap and said he'd book one from there.

The mess in the flat didn't give the impression that he had a life. It looked rather as though he was a middle-aged man who lived like a student. He lit a lamp and a couple of candles. He put a match to a Firelog in the grate and opened a bottle of wine. He told her to choose a record. She flipped through them and didn't seem to recognise the ones she had bought for him. She told him she hadn't listened to music for years and sat at the table beside him. He rolled a joint and offered it to her. She took a small drag and left it hanging between her fingers. She put it to her lips again. It had gone out. I can't remember how to do this, she said. He relit it and passed it back to her. She shook her head.

He pushed the plans towards her. Is this for my garden? she said. He had written the plant names in Latin. *Euphorbia hortensis. Alchemilla mollis. Veratrum album.*

Yeah. I had a pampas grass in there, but I rubbed it out. Your neighbours might get the wrong idea about you.

How come?

It's the plant swingers used to put in their gardens in the seventies, he said.

We already decided on the planting. Low maintenance, vaguely Mediterranean was what we said.

But you have great soil, a loam you can grow anything in.

We don't have time.

Would your husband not look after the garden for
you?

We're busy people. Clive's away all week and I'm flat
out with work and Roo. We're going to get a gardener to
come in a couple of hours a week to keep it tidy.

They sat in silence looking at the plans.

I don't usually do garden maintenance, he said eventually, but I'm free on Saturday mornings.

You don't seriously think you can come and hang
around our home every weekend. It's weird enough as
it is. *Our home.* She stood abruptly and put on her jacket.
I'm sorry I didn't answer your letters, but my parents
were a bit anti, to put it mildly. They would have bloody
killed me. And I was so fucked up about the accident I
needed to stay away.

The morning sun was low, the sky a searing blue. He
drove to the garden centre with the visor down. He
loaded a pallet with plants, the ones from Robbie's plan,
and called to the locksmith's kiosk in the hardware section before driving back towards town.

When he got to Niamh's house after ten, he let himself
into the kitchen. He made a coffee and stood on the mat

to drink it. The cleaner came out of the utility room with a basket of wet laundry. He watched her sling the clothes over the pulley: jeans and the grey crew-necked top Niamh had worn the previous night. Peachy knickers and a matching bra that he never got to see.

Niamh says you must give the key back, she said.

He handed it over and left his cup in the sink.

He worked through until two when the cleaner left and let himself in with the key he had cut earlier. He went into the living room and poured himself a Scotch from a bottle with a hand-written number on it. It tasted like turf. He carried it down the hall to the master bedroom and lay on Clive's side of the bed. He got under the covers and reached his arms out as though he was reaching for Niamh. The bedlinen was expensive, soft where it brushed his skin. He turned the pockets of his jeans inside out and dredged the sheet with crumbs of soil, writhing around to grind them in. There was a book on the bedside table, a collection of *Speeches That Changed the World*. He read the speech JFK made in Berlin. *Ich bin ein Berliner*, he said aloud; he had read somewhere that it meant *I am a doughnut*.

Outside, he sprinkled bark chips over the sheeting, raking them out until there was no trace of the plastic. He took each plant out of its casing and rubbed at the root ball to loosen it. He put the plants in the ground and bedded them down, patting the earth until all you could see was what you wanted to see: stem and branch, the nubs of leaf buds. In the places the sun had touched, the soil was warm. He loaded his tools into the van and drove home.

Mrs Ferguson was in the hallway. She had on the type of cotton cap that was popular with chemotherapy patients and old ladies who had never had to do their own hair.

I'm not a bit well, she said.

Ah no.

I might come over later. Unless you're expecting company.

You don't miss much, he said. I'll be back by six. All on my lonesome.

BRITTLE THINGS

She turned from the stove and made the word again. *Mum.*

Ferdia brought his fist down on the Matchbox cars he had queued along the hearthrug. They hurtled across the floor, a motorway pile-up in miniature.

Mum, Ferdia. Mum, said Ciara. He began to line the cars up again. Ciara turned back to the stock pot. She knew the order without looking. Red Ferrari, blue BMW, black Mercedes, orange Beetle, burgundy 2CV, cream Mini Cooper. With a long-handled strainer, she dredged through straggles of boiled herbs and removed the cooked crabs.

Before Ferdia, she had never really thought about words. They had been written or read, said or unsaid. Now they were made, with all the effort and craft implicit in that. The speech therapist had told her to talk to Ferdia. Say anything to him, natter away, she said. And don't be worrying about coaching him in particular words. Just keep talking.

At first Ciara had felt foolish; without any response it was like talking to herself. Soon she found herself sharing confidences, as if he was a girlfriend. Sometimes she talked to Ferdia about Dan, wishing aloud he would listen to her, believe her. She fretted now that Ferdia's first words, if they ever came, would be words against his father. Sometimes she gave him a running commentary of what she was doing. *I'm dropping four crabs into the pot, now, Ferdia. Fine big ones they are too.* Mostly, she ignored the advice and said a particular word.

Mum.

Ferdia bashed the cars again. There was a scratch from the plastic crate at Ciara's feet. A small crab was wedged on its side. It was missing a claw. It twitched its remaining pincers then was still. She pulled it out quickly and dropped it into the pot, then threw another four after it. The remaining crabs in the crate fizzled.

Dan had been at the pier. The catch had been good for weeks. Too good, he said; the lobsters were fetching a low price. The crabs that found their way into the creels were brought home to Ciara now. Before, Dan had twisted their claws off and tossed the bodies into the sea. Ciara hated to think of what they felt beneath their shells as they tumbled through the grey-green water off the pier, where they lay fettered in bladderwrack until they turned putrid. Dan delighted in her horror.

They're crabs, love. What else would they be doing? They'd hardly be finding a cure for cancer. He called her love when he thought she was being ridiculous.

Ciara prepared them in the galley kitchen off the sitting room in the cottage. She worked with the radio on, talk radio that kept her company as she cracked and picked and flaked. She dressed whole crabs, finishing them with stripes of brown and white meat, a flower pattern of lemon and parsley and black peppercorns laid on top. She weighed half-pound pouches of flaked white crabmeat and big polythene bags of claws. Twice a week she delivered to a fancy food shop in town. She lied to Dan about the time it took. She stood at the hob until her neck was stiff, her fingertips livid cushions of tiny pink wounds. Still, last week she had earned enough to pay for another private appointment for Ferdia with the speech therapist. Private and secret.

She threw a posy of fennel and lovage into the pot and sidestepped Ferdia and his cars to reach the television. The DVD was coming to an end. She managed to replay the cartoon before Ferdia heard the theme tune. It was about creatures that live on the ocean floor who answer to names like Chowder. Dan had bought it, kneeling down to play it as soon as he brought it into the house.

Ferdia'll learn loads of shit about the sea from this. Really get into it.

Ferdia was into it, all right. Into it in the way he was into having two fish fingers at Buzz Lightyear's left shoulder and a potato waffle balanced on Woody's knees on his *Toy Story* plate. Or like he was into wearing his

Spider-Man pyjamas every single day, so that the stitching had dissolved and the fabric had faded to a pale coral
colour. The DVD had become part of the scaffolding of
Ferdia's life. It played from dawn to dusk without ever
reaching the end. The closing titles sent him into parox-
ysms of fury. The last time he had seen them he had run
at her and pushed his head into her gut, knocking her
on to the couch. She didn't tell Dan; she knew what
he'd say.

The parenting, love. It's all about the parenting.

Ferdia was happiest at home. Outside, the world was
an assault of the unfamiliar, where strangers punched
at their car horns, stuck instruments in his ears, cut his
hair. In the cottage, Ciara could keep his life running on a
loop, so that he wouldn't feel startled. He was long, like
Dan, and strong. His rages were increasingly savage and
Ciara found it hard to quell them. Dan seemed to be able
to manage him, or at least had the muscles to scoop him
up and take him away when he went off on one. But Dan
rarely strayed beyond the rough triangle from cottage
to pier to Maisie's pub, leaving Ciara to negotiate town
with Ferdia.

Dan came and went throughout the day, calling *Wilma,
I'm home* as he came in the back door, kissing Ciara as if
she was a mum in a sitcom. He seemed to fill the place.
His voice was sonorous, like the man who did the voice-
overs for blockbuster movie trailers. He put thought into

the clothes he wore; his fleeces and body warmers were North Face, his checked shirts A&F. Apple Crumble and Fish, he liked to say. When he sat in a chair, his limbs slanted across the room, something languid in the fold of his hands across his lap, in the spread of his arm over the back of the couch. The tip of his middle finger was missing at the first joint, the stub chunky, the only part of his body he was shy about. Ciara liked how it jarred with the louche perfection of the rest of him.

He would brew coffee for them, bringing his to the other room, where he knelt on the floor beside his son. Ciara watched this scene countless times from the doorway, willing Ferdia to raise his head. Good man, Dan would say when cars were lined up. Good man. He'd watch him with such tenderness she had to turn away. He put Ferdia to bed at night, and she would listen to him read, the pause as he asked the boy to repeat the last line. The … come on, buddy. The End. A scrape of want in his voice she knew was in hers too, willing the child to answer.

At the pier they called him Dan the Man. His grandfather had been the harbourmaster, and the other men liked the stories he had, and the lingo picked up from the Marine Biology course he never finished. They rolled cigarettes, mackerel and ling slithering on the slipway, while Dan made them laugh. He found markets for their hauls, for unfashionable fish they had once given away.

He used words like responsible and sustainable to talk his way into a couple of shops. A man from the town who went around the farmers' markets with a fish truck bought everything else, convinced by the 'fishing for generations' spiel Dan thought of during a lock-in at Maisie's.

He even got money for the pollock, the fishermen said. Dan the Man got us money for the pollock.

Ciara turned off the gas and pushed the pot to the back of the cooker. She brought Ferdia outside. Dan had made her a polytunnel in the shelter of the New Zealand flax that bordered the west side of the garden. She tended herbs and leaves and vegetables she had nurtured from seed, old-fashioned varieties she grew for their pretty names and colours. Between the lines of mizuna and rocket there were shocks of calendula and borage and viola. She gave Ferdia a nasturtium flower and showed him the squashes in fairy-tale shapes that snaked around the dwarf pear tree in the middle of the tunnel. She came out damp from the condensation and stood in the garden with Ferdia in her arms. Great clouds had skated in from the sea, mottling the lawn and surrounding fields into light or shade, and were moving away, dragging their shadows behind them. It was overwhelming, living under skies like that.

She brought Ferdia into the bathroom. She rubbed at his face and hands with a wipe and pulled his trainer pants down. She sat him on the toilet and gave him a bread-stick. A pebble of a stool plopped into the water. He was getting really into breadsticks. Some days he ate an entire packet of them, but she didn't know how else to get him to do things. They were making him constipated and the small victories she had won with toilet training were lost when she put him on the seat and nothing happened. The lack of hygiene appalled her, when she let herself think about it: feeding a child while he sat on the toilet.

She put her head inside her top and sniffed. She should have showered. Dan had woken her at dawn, scrabbing at the soles of her feet with his toenails.

What are you at?

Foreplay, they call it.

She put his hand inside her knickers and pressed the stump inside her. Afterwards she had dressed without washing, wanting the taint of him on her skin. Salt and fish. Diesel and tobacco. Now that she had to go out she felt filthy. She persuaded Ferdia into the buggy with another breadstick, sprayed deodorant under her arms and changed her top. They left for Maisie's.

Dan had walked the long acre, a strip of field that ran from the side of their cottage to the back of the pub. The thick grass had been tramped flat by men's boots, though it was stony in places, too uneven for the buggy. Instead, she turned right at the gate and began the half-mile trek along the road. It was the last Sunday in August, humid and warm, as it had been all summer. She and Ferdia cast gaunt shadows on the tarmac. She hadn't been for a walk for over a week. The rain had kept her indoors; the rain and the crabs and Ferdia.

The Mangans were their nearest neighbours. Their hedge drooped rosehips and the red and green colours of Mayo flapped from the flagpole they'd put up for the papal visit in '79. It was a tradition Mossy Mangan had begun in the eighties, to annoy Dan's father after a dispute over drainage. Breda Mangan was at the gate.

That's the summer over.

Maybe. It's gorgeous today, though. You've some colour, Breda. Were you away?

That fella wouldn't bring me to Bundoran.

Your hydrangeas are lovely. I only have the pink ones everyone has.

I put stuff in the soil to turn them blue.

I might copy you.

And how are you, little man? Breda bent over the pram. Ferdia bucked and banged his head against the side of the hood. Ciara quickly gave him a breadstick.

He's a McLoughlin, anyways, said Breda. She was looking at Ciara.

He's like Dan, all right.

Maisie's, is it?

Just for one or two. Not very exciting.

I know well. I might be up after you, sure.

The fine weather had drawn walkers and Sunday drivers to the thirsty-looking picnic tables outside the pub. Stools from the lounge had been taken outside and were lined against the front wall. At first Ciara couldn't see Dan. He came loping, then, from round the side of the pub. He was with Marcus, a young Dubliner whose family owned a holiday home near the pier. Dan leaned into her, the grass she caught on his breath already dilating his pupils.

You stink, said Ciara, turning away. Dan put his mouth to her ear.

You're a bit ripe yourself, he said. Did you even change those drawers you had on you? He kissed her, full and fast. He knelt in front of Ferdia.

How's my wee Spider-Man?

A young woman joined them. She was dressed in light knitwear and Hunter wellingtons, long brown hair fading to honey at the ends. She stepped forward with her hand out. Ciara, is it? I'm Hannah. She looked into the buggy. And this must be Ferdia! Oh my God, those curls! Your dad is totally mad about you.

Ciara was already handing over a breadstick when the bucking started. He thrashed once or twice and calmed when the food was in his mouth. She felt the couple's eyes on her. It must have looked like she was training a puppy.

My shout, said Marcus.

Ah no, we'll stay on our own, said Dan, though they all knew Marcus would buy the round. Dan had let Marcus leave his boat at the pier. Payment seemed to be coming in the form of pints and the odd wrap of coke.

Ciara asked for a pint of Guinness. Hannah asked for a gin and tonic. Marcus went inside and Dan carried over two stools. Their tapestry-patterned upholstery was soiled to a dark sheen that caught the sun. Hannah hesitated then sat. She twisted around on her stool to face Ciara.

I bought some of your stuff from that deli in town. It was amazing.

Ah, thanks.

We had it in front of the fire with a bottle of wine.

Ciara put a Mickey Mouse soother into Ferdia's mouth and rocked the buggy gently by the handle, her eyes on the ground, aware of the plastic plug in Ferdia's face, a sign of her ineptitude. Marcus came back with the drinks. He handed Hannah hers first.

Yum, she said.

Dan took a drink from his pint. Your health, he said and Ciara saw Hannah turn to him, as if she hadn't noticed him before. The voice. It scarcely mattered what Dan said. It was the voice.

Dan had learned how to use the voice. He had learned how to craft his own poor judgement into parables, casting himself as victim, as somehow hapless. He told tales of calamity, of catastrophe. Fishermen are at home with catastrophe. Ciara wondered what stories he had told them. There was the wee trawler in Alaska he had bought a share in that was used for a drug run by a fella he hardly knew, then impounded. And the lake he had rented down in the midlands to rear Arctic char that got contaminated with shite that seeped from a TD's pig farm.

Hannah poked at her drink with a straw.

Are you from the area too, Ciara?

I'm from Galway.

How did you meet?

On a day trip to Inishmurray with college.

There's a story, said Dan.

There's always a story, said Marcus.

So. I'm doing runs to the island while Lar Henry is getting the hip done, said Dan.

Jesus, said Ciara.

A rake of students get on the boat, full of it about the monastery and everything. The shite talking out of them has to be heard to be believed. One of them is quiet. She's sitting at the back of the boat and is slow to get off. I can tell she's scared.

I was not scared.

You were. Anyway. I hold my hand out and she steps off. She looks up at me. Her eyes are grey-green, like the sea. And she's pale, really pale. Black hair. Like a fucking selkie or something. So I'm kind of checking her out, and she doesn't seem to be in any hurry to go after the others. Then she does this strange thing, right. She puts her hand on my heart and lowers her head. Like this. He closed his eyes and looked down.

You're some bollocks, said Ciara.

What then? said Marcus. The people at the next table had stopped talking.

She vomits. All over my boots. Sick as a dog, she was. I brought them all in here afterwards for a brandy and talked the knickers off her.

Fuck's sake, Ciara said, but she was laughing too.

So have you been here ever since? said Hannah.

Pretty much, Ciara said, lifting her pint, aware of her chipped nails and scaly knuckles. Hannah's hands were slender, the skin pearly. Ciara watched her shake out her hair. The cut and colour were so expensive it looked as though she hadn't had her hair done at all. In the magazines they called it baliage, the fading through of the colour; round here they called it a dip dye, which sounded like something you'd go to a vet for. Marcus wound his fingers around Hannah's belt and pulled her to him. Ciara looked at Dan, ready to raise an eyebrow, but he was at the next table, saying something in a low voice that made them roar with laughter.

So, what do you do for kicks, Ciara? said Marcus. He was trying to be friendly. Part of her was ashamed that the dreariness of her life was being acknowledged. Another part was relieved to be in the company of adults. Dan appeared beside her.

Ciara does the full Peig Sayers on it.

Really? said Hannah.

Fuck, yeah. She was out this morning putting blue-stone on her potatoes to keep the blight from them. Peig, with her spuds and her bubbling pot and her hens, said Dan. It was mean of him to mention the hens. They had been flittered by a fox one night, all six of them. The only one to survive had been like something you'd see in a Wes Craven film, he said, after he had wrung its neck. He had called her love that morning too.

How do you get the time to do all that? Baby on board, to boot, said Hannah.

Ferdia plays away all day. He's no bother, said Dan.

I'm going to try to get him a place in school next year, said Ciara. She looked at Ferdia. His face was pressed to the side of the buggy, his hair coiling away from his cheeks.

Apparently it's really hard to get a school place in Dublin too, said Hannah. Ciara let the misunderstanding take. The local school had two teachers and only eigh-teen pupils and was constantly struggling to keep the numbers up to stay open.

We've been talking about home schooling, said Dan.

Wow. You pair really have this alternative-lifestyle thing sorted.

Dan had mooted the idea weeks ago, but Ciara had been so against it she couldn't believe he was bringing it up now. Marcus twitched his thumb in the direction of the pub and he and Dan went around the side again.

How would you even do it? said Hannah. Do you have to be a teacher or something, or is there a syllabus to follow?

We didn't get that far with it.

He's just divine, Hannah said. Like a cherub from a painting. How old is he?

He's four. Ciara waited for Hannah to say something. She was too polite for that, though Ciara watched something cross her face, a dawning on her. Ferdia would be five in a week. How would Hannah have reacted to the higher figure?

Ciara knew the milestones he should have reached by now. She could rhyme them off. She had spent hours on the computer, but Dan had seen the search history and been angry. Everything gets a fucking label these days, he said. You can't just be. Now she went to the library once a week, picking up a couple of books for herself, books she didn't have time to read. They had become a cover for her, a way of getting into town for a couple of hours. She sat in a booth in the converted church that housed the library, under the mural of *The Battle of the Books*, and typed in words. It was like a game of I spy, her worst fears for Ferdia as the guesses. Is it something beginning with ... dys? Is it something beginning with ... aut? Often the words were completed by the computer and she wondered about the other mothers nearby, sitting at their kitchen tables, in cafes, at their desks, tensed over their phones, trying to figure out what was wrong with their children. Sometimes Ciara typed phrases in, symptoms really, but couldn't find a single condition it might be. She read a post in a forum from a woman who said she had been told her son had global difficulties. It sounded grandly disastrous, like climate change or the War on Terror.

Ciara had been the first of her friends to get pregnant. She had been so excited she had asked them to tell her the baby's sex at the scan. She had loved the swell of him inside her, the sureness she had felt. The girls had joked about the child she would have. He'll have the gift of the gab, anyway. I wonder will he come out and speak to you with the God voice, like Dan. Her friends had followed her quickly. Ciara oohed and aahed over their children, their dry-at-night victories, the first words, the malapropisms, the swearing that had to be ignored. How she'd give anything for Ferdia to tell her to go away and fuck herself. Their babies had thickened and hardened into toddlers, then pre-school children, with best friends and favourite songs. They attended a purpose-built Montessori school that held exhibitions of the children's art and had a graduation ceremony at the end of each year. Lorraine's Isobel had said a poem at the Feis. Claire's Jake loved her to infinity and beyond. Ciara looked sometimes at her faraway boy and wondered what dreadful thing she had done. She feared she had jinxed them, that she shouldn't have wanted a son so badly, a boy for Dan.

The girls asked around Ferdia, never about him. They enquired about Dan and the cottage and the hens and the bubbling pot, but never named her son. When she talked about him, they listened and smiled. God love him, they murmured. They told her she needed to get out more, that she was an amazing mum. It seemed to her that 'you're amazing' meant 'how do you tolerate your life?'

Hannah put the straw to her lips again and Ciara saw her glance at Ferdia. In sleep he looked untroubled; his lips parted, beyond them the crimson promise of the mouth that had never made a single word. Could Ciara tell Hannah? My son has never hugged me, never kissed me. When he falls, he picks himself up and walks away, never comes to me for comfort. He sits on the floor and plays with the same toys in the same order, over and over. He is not fully toilet trained. He walks on his tiptoes. He doesn't reply when I speak his name. In a week, he will be five years old. And his father thinks there is nothing wrong with him. Who would want to hear that?

Dan and Marcus came back giggling. Dan was describing a field, the one that bordered the lodge house at the entrance to the castle.

Loads of shrooms up there. Lovely buzz, a handful of those and a few pints, he was saying.

Hannah frowned and crossed her arms over herself. The sun had moved around the back of the building and they were in the shade. We should go inside, she said. It's bloody Baltic.

Dan pushed ahead with the buggy, Ciara carrying their pints. In the lounge, the television above the till was showing a football match. The barman came through the saloon doors from the bar, dirty glasses between his fingers, and whinnied at the score. The fishermen were sitting along the counter. They had a word for Ciara, scarcely a nod for Marcus, and a double-take for Hannah. Dan put a hand on Lar Henry's shoulder and whispered something. Lar glanced at Marcus, who was waiting for his change.

So, back to this home-schooling idea. Dan says you've a degree, said Hannah.

Yeah, in Celtic Studies. Nothing that would qualify me to educate a child.

It's about a way of thinking, babe. You can choose what to teach him, said Dan. He seemed to appear beside her whenever she talked about Ferdia.

The fishermen were apt to complain about the teenagers who slunk around the lounge and monopolised the pool table. Lar leaned back on his bar stool theatrically, to watch a young blonde girl take a shot. There was a tattoo on her back, a tendril of foliage snaking towards the crack of her arse. The other men laughed, and the girl was suddenly abashed, handing her cue to one of the boys. She sat down by a table in the corner. Lar turned back and ordered a pint, his last before his wife came to bring him home for a roast dinner. He called her Duchess. *Duchess is a fucking lady.*

That young one is mortified, said Ciara.

Dan shrugged. Sure, look. She'll get over it.

In the buggy, Ferdia stretched and cried out, a stunted, mawing sound. The men at the bar scarcely looked, knowing it was Dan's child who had made the noise. Around the pool table there was silence, a couple of the boys drinking their pints and watching. Dan knelt and began to open the straps.

Ah, don't, Dan, leave him, said Ciara.

He's grand. Needs to stretch the legs, don't you, son? He kissed his hair and lifted him high, then perched him at his elbow. It reminded Ciara of a ventriloquist she had seen on television, holding a rosy-cheeked dummy with an inscrutable expression. She was filled with disgust at herself for the thought. Out of the buggy, long legs swinging down almost to Dan's knee, shoulders stiff, Ferdia could have been six or seven. His pull-up nappy was plump, a crescent of piss under his left buttock darkening the Spider-Man costume to its original colour. He writhed and moaned until Dan put him standing on the floor, rocking unsteadily in place on his toes. Ciara plunged her hand into her bag, groping about for the packet of bread-sticks. She pulled out the cellophane wrapper, and delved again, this time finding one. It had a couple of hairs on it, and a smudge of ink from the corner of the lining, where a biro had leaked a few weeks before. She began to rub at it, saw something pass between Marcus and Hannah.

We might head on, she told Dan. He didn't seem to hear and went to the bar. Ferdia saw the breadstick and opened and closed his fists, rocking faster. She thrust it at him, hoping Hannah wasn't looking. It fell on the floor. Ferdia's face twisted and his voice rose. Dan turned from the bar and threw open his arms. Ciara knelt to pick up the bread-stick. Her jeans made an unsticking sound as she got off the carpet, like Velcro being pulled apart. She didn't want to give the breadstick to Ferdia but didn't know what else to do. Dan came just as she was handing it over.

The fuck are you at?

He's about to go nuts, Dan, please can we go?

You have to get him used to it, train him up.

Ferdia was almost bouncing on his tiptoes, a wildness in his eyes.

Billy Elliot! He'd make a great dancer, said Hannah.

Ferdia hurled himself at Ciara, a plaintive, bestial noise coming from him. She felt her hands go up to shield herself, felt his shoulder at her kidney. Dan put his pint down and swept him up. Everyone was watching, except Lar and the boys, who were intent on the television. Ciara thought she saw a curl of a smile on the face of the girl who had been shamed away from the pool table. Ferdia flailed about, Dan hushing him.

Come on, he said to Ciara. His voice was sharp.

Good luck, man. You too, Ciara. And I'm sure we'll see the Quiet Man again soon, Marcus said.

Dan turned slowly to face him. He's called Ferdia. My son's name is Ferdia.

Shit. I was only messing. I wasn't even sure there was anything wrong.

Christ, Marcus, said Hannah. Look, I'm sorry too. He's a gorgeous child. We don't know a thing about kids.

Outside, the tables were still strewn with abandoned glasses and bottles. They started home through the long acre, Dan carrying Ferdia, Ciara pushing the empty buggy. Dan set Ferdia on the ground. He went ahead of them, jerking along the path with tight, uncertain steps. Ciara tugged Dan's sleeve.

You OK?

Those assholes.

I don't think they meant anything by it.

Ferdia had stalled and was jigging again on his toes. Dan stopped to look at her. I thought it would sort itself out. That he'd catch up, just start talking. It's not happening, though, is it?

Ciara didn't answer. She didn't need to.

Does it hurt him, do you think? Walking on his tiptoes like that.

It hurts him to walk like we do.

In the distance, warped oblongs of rape and grass edged the stony headland. The field that bordered the castle had been ploughed and was ridged, like brown corduroy.

That field you were telling him about. It's dug up, said Ciara.

And there are never any mushrooms there. I suppose you think I'm petty.

A bit. He's an awful dick, though.

They reached the stile at the end of the lane, Dan helping Ferdia over first, then Ciara with the buggy. Breda Mangan pulled herself up from where she was kneeling, a scorch of red dahlias behind her.

How's the best-looking family for twenty miles?

I'm like a bag of shite, Ciara said.

Indeed and you're not. You did all right, Dan McLoughlin.

I suppose I did, Dan said.

Any craic up there today?

I've more craic at home with this pair.

In the cottage, Ciara changed Ferdia. Dan put on the DVD and lit a fire. She laid a clean tea towel on the worktop and took out her hammer, picks and spikes. From the doorway she watched them. Dan was lying on the floor beside Ferdia, propped on his elbow, careful not to touch the white line. The fire belched phosphorous flames, and the cars lay jumbled on the mat. Ciara picked up a crab. It was the one from earlier, with only one claw. From the other room, the cartoon people at the bottom of the sea danced a hornpipe and she heard the tinny click of metal on metal as Ferdia lined the cars up. Ciara put the damaged crab aside and chose a different one. She brought her hammer down just as Ferdia's fist sent the cars flying across the floor.

Mum, Ferdia, said Dan. Say Mum.

SPARING THE HEATHER

Each time she came it felt less like her house. There was a pot soaking on the hob, a mealy ribbon peeling away from its sides, the dregs of a stew of lentils or beans; Hugh only ate meat he had killed himself. The kitchen dresser had been rearranged. She had left ornaments behind, things she neither liked nor used. A pair of glass candlesticks, an Aynsley china vase. Six dark blue pottery wine goblets too heavy to drink from. A pewter ashtray. Hugh had moved them aside and they were in hasty clusters in the corners of the shelves. There were photographs in their place, faded Polaroids in assorted frames.

The kitchen table was covered with sheets of newspaper. Hugh's shotgun was dismantled on the pages: barrel, shaft and fore-end laid out neatly, the cleaning paraphernalia less so. There were twisted rags, a roll of blue paper towels. Brass-tipped mahogany rods and their attachments: a couple of jags, a phosphor bronze brush, a tiny wool mop. An open can of lead and copper solvent that smelled like pear drops, a closed can of gun oil. The rent was in an envelope on the dresser. Mairead put it in her bag and went down the hall to Hugh's room.

Normally the dog rested his chin on the bed and waited. Today he was agitated, skirring about. He was a wire-haired fox terrier called Arthur, with a coarse beard and eyes that watered like an old man's. As Hugh finished, Mairead felt a tongue across the sole of her foot.

Bloody dog, she said, wiping her heel on the sheets.

Hugh's thigh was lying heavily across her hip and she had to push him off to get up. He switched on the bedside lamp and watched her dress. She turned away. She hated the silvery pucker of her stretch marks, how flat her tits looked without the chicken fillets she put in her bra. The crêpey slump of her skin. Not that he seemed to mind. He was always looking at her, leaving the light on so he could see what he was doing, watching as he put himself inside her.

I can give you a lift up the road, he said.

Will you fuck. I'll see you later on.

She left the house through the back door. It needed a coat of varnish, the window frames too. She'd asked Brendan to paint it, but he said for the pittance they were getting off Hugh in rent he could sing for it. The wind was coming from the east and walking uphill against it she felt weak and small. She stopped at the top of the road where the glen came into sight. It was florid with heather, blackened in strips where Hugh had begun the burning. The tents the Garda search team had erected were at the foot of the north slope. For weeks they had been combing the moor, crossing back and forth in high-vis jackets. Today the only movement was the sporadic flapping of white canvas. It was Sunday.

Brendan was loading the car in the driveway when she got home.

We need to leave in an hour, he said.

I'm only back from a walk. I don't know if I'll bother.

There's a meal booked for after. The rest of the wives'll be there.

Is that supposed to make me want to go?

I don't know, Mairead. Go or don't go.

She went upstairs to their room and tilted back the long mirror. There was gun oil on her face, a smear that started at her chin and disappeared under her collar. She took her clothes off. The mark stopped abruptly at her left nipple. She heard Brendan's feet on the stairs and went into the bathroom. She took her time getting ready, imagining him sitting in the car waiting for her, fuming.

When she came down Brendan was strapped into the driver's seat with the engine running, his elbow resting on the open window. There was pop music playing on the car radio but his fingers were tapping in time to some unheard tune, one of those melancholic pipe solos he liked to listen to. She got in beside him and turned the volume up. They went the half mile or so to the glen without speaking.

Half the village was in the lay-by. Brendan got out and began to empty the boot. Mairead pulled down the visor. Her make-up was caked and patchy where Hugh's chin had scraped her. He was near the stile, wearing the jacket with all the pockets he called a jerkin. Arthur was nervous, running at cars as they arrived, scudding against legs and knees. He came cantering towards her, butting her hard in the crotch and knocking her against the car. Brendan glared at her, as if she had done something to encourage the animal. Hugh gave a sharp whistle and Arthur went back to him. The dog could give them away, carrying on like that.

She followed Brendan towards the stile. He put his hand on Hugh's shoulder. Well, big man, he said. Not a bad turnout.

Not bad at all. He clapped his hands together and they all turned to look at him. Right, he called. Let's go.

Someone said, Tally-ho. Someone else laughed. Hugh didn't seem to have heard. He wasn't meant to.

He crossed first, swinging a long leg over the wire fence. Brendan followed him in close, quick movements. She hadn't seen them together since the day Hugh moved in. Brendan had objected to the Gun Club's plan to hire a gamekeeper, but when it was clear it was going ahead he behaved as though it had been his idea, offering the house at low rent, showing him around. He bought a bottle of whiskey and asked Mairead to come with him to meet their new tenant. Hugh made them hot toddies and talked about the estate he had worked on in Scotland. When Mairead called the following week to collect the rent, Hugh was at the kitchen table, buffing his boots with dubbin. Radio 4 was playing low. He said he often went days without speaking to anyone and thanked her for coming. The next week he didn't say anything at all and they had sex on one of the kitchen chairs.

They crossed into the low field. Underfoot the earth was soft, the layer of dab a wet, shallow wadding that sat on the bedrock, tufted with pond sedge and reed. Brendan and Hugh were four or five feet apart. There was a difference in how they moved across the land. Her husband hunched and wary. The Englishman loose-limbed, easeful.

There were crows in the sky. One dropped into their range, and both men aimed. Hugh fired first, his shoulders jerking back on the recoil. The bird flung its wings wide, tumbling over itself as it fell. Arthur ran to get it and came back with the body swinging slick and limp from his jaws. He dropped it at Hugh's feet.

Boggy sedges gave way to cross-leaved heath, to bilberry and wintergreen. They were climbing, the tilt of the mountain straining Mairead's knees, her shins.

A narrow trail bent upwards to the tor, beaten flat by men's boots; one by one they took it. The path was uneven, and Mairead had to take high, deliberate steps to avoid a nub of rock, a clump of scutch grass. The fields and the village appeared to flatten out below them.

The path opened and they were on the moor. Listen, said Hugh and they all stopped where they were. There, he said. The call of the male. Some of the others were nodding. All Mairead could hear was the beat of wind in the air, the screaks of crows.

This close, the heather was a tangled weave of woody stalks and small purple flowers, without the dark blush it had from a distance. Across the moor were blackened strips, uniform in shape and size. Hugh led them to the one he had burned first, in the autumn when he had just arrived. He said that grouse need old heather to hide in and young heather to feed on; that controlled burning yields both. Small green shoots were already poking from the charred mess.

He turned suddenly, crossing in light strides towards a dense bank of heather. He aimed into the thicket. There was a glimpse of ginger fur, and a fox slipped away over the hanging rock and down the western slope. I've been trying to get that bugger for weeks, he said.

He wouldn't be the first Brit out-foxed round here, someone said. Hugh glanced around. This time he had heard.

He walked a few paces and laid down his gun. He lowered his shoulder and let his backpack slide on to the ground. He took out kerosene, a lighter, a rag. Brendan was beside him as he started the fire, the rest of the party keeping back, ten or twelve feet away. There was a leap of orange flame that died to a smoulder. The wind came up and it caught, parched stems snapping in the heat, smoky and fragrant. It was the scent she knew from Hugh's skin and hair, from his daft-looking jerkin. They watched the fire burn out, and he stamped his boots vigorously around the edges.

They turned back towards the trail. Her foot bounced off something sleek that made a tight, high sound like a baby's toy. A crow from an earlier cull, squeaking with maggots.

Cars from both sides of the border were lined along the road outside the hotel, the northern ones clean and new. Inside, there were gangs of sweaty children roaming the room, mothers looking under tables for jackets and shoes. Along one wall, several tables had been pushed together and covered with white cloths; the women in the party allowed a waitress to usher them to it. They took their seats slowly, changing places, arranging their gaudy waterproofs on the backs of their chairs, pouring water for each other. The men went to the bar and Mairead followed them.

Brendan was at the counter with his back to her. He handed pints to the men as they were put up. Hugh was standing slightly to the side.

Hello, he said quietly.

Hiya, she said.

Brendan turned from the bar. There's wine on the table.

I saw that. I'll have a gin and slimline.

He turned back to the counter.

Did you enjoy today? Hugh asked her.

It was all right, she said. I got in my ten thousand steps.

She had found it brutal. The men spreading out across the heath. The sudden burst of fire in the heather. The dead crows and the harried fox.

Brendan handed her the drink and leaned back against the bar. He took a sip of his pint and looked off into the middle distance, his features arranging themselves into the ridiculous *seanachaí* face he wore on occasions like this. He started to speak. The old name for the place was *mointean cearca fraoigh*, grouse moor, he said. The heather had once twitched with the fat russet birds, he went on, the coarse call of the male, *co co co co mo chlaidh, mo chlaidh?* who, who, who, who goes there? crackling across the glen. Mairead had an impulse to laugh or scream or pour the gin over her head. She looked at Hugh, hoping to exchange a sneer or an eye-roll, but he was rapt. One day, Brendan went on, when he was nine or ten, his father brought him up the glen. They met men from the north coming down the path, stooped under the weight of the sacks of dead birds they'd slung over their backs. From the edge of the heath they watched them leave. Saw a thin red line of blood dribbling down the trail in their wake. He and his father went on to the moor and listened for the call – he lowered his voice for this part – but there was nothing. The grouse were gone. The story never changed, always the same words in the same order, the same conspiratorial delivery. So faithful to the first time she'd heard it she didn't believe it any more. Obliteration was so much slower than that. A dying-off in tiny increments.

Brendan loved this sort of story, of men from the north or the east laying waste to his heritage. Once, they had stayed in a hotel down the country. In the hallway there were taxidermied animals in glass cases. A plaque claimed that one of the palsied, glassy-eyed creatures was the last Irish wolf. Mairead overheard an American tourist say it was an Alaskan one. She went to the spa to book her free treatment, leaving Brendan to take photographs of it.

Dreadful. Utter barbarians, Hugh said. Mairead drained the last of her drink. Brendan moved away to talk to the other men and Hugh stood to buy a round. When he passed her the glass, he bowed and fanned his arm towards her in a rolling wave, like a medieval knight. She felt heat spreading across her face.

What are you doing? she said.

Being chivalrous.

You needn't bother your head.

He didn't see.

Everyone else in the place did.

They joined the others at the long table. Brendan sat at the head, with Hugh and Mairead either side of him. The waitress came. Hugh asked about the vegetarian option. She said it was a noodle dish that she couldn't pronounce the name of.

I don't know if I can face another Irish stir-fry, he said and ordered a roast beef dinner without the meat.

He lifted a bottle of white wine and filled Mairead's glass. He hadn't asked her what colour she wanted. He sucked in his breath, realising his mistake. A good guess, he said. He offered wine to the others. Brendan swilled beer around his glass and watched.

It was something else, up there today. Hearing the call again, said Brendan.

I hear a different call, you know, said Hugh.

What would that be?

Go back, go back, go back back back.

They must know you're English, said Brendan and punched him lightly on the arm. Do you mind being up there all day on your own?

I'm used to it. I like the fresh air. The quiet. And it's not that lonely. I've got to know the guys from the search team.

The Guards? said Brendan.

Yes. Sometimes I have tea with them.

You'll be the only one who'll miss them when they're gone, so. They've this place on the news every other day, making us look bad.

They aren't going anywhere.

Is that so?

They're going to concentrate the search on the western slope.

That's very specific.

Talk went around the table. *It'd be a relief for the family if they find his remains. It must be dreadful for them. All those rumours. They say his body was ground up in a meat processing plant. I heard he didn't die at all. He was driven away by British intelligence and given a new identity.*

Truth will out, I suppose, said Hugh and bent over his plate. He went at his food, slashing it into small pieces, mixing it briskly. When they were alone she liked his eagerness. Now he seemed schoolboyish.

They were served a 'trio' of wobbly desserts and tea and coffee from large stainless-steel pots. People began to leave. Mairead refused a lift home from a neighbour. The room was almost empty when they left the table and went to sit at the bar. Hugh went outside to give Arthur some water. She asked Brendan for a brandy. She had drunk most of the bottle of white wine and her teeth were furry with sugar. He usually remarked on how much she had drunk, but he gave it to her without comment. What was he at?

Hugh came back in and sat beside Brendan. They talked about sport. Hugh about cricket, how he always bought the *Sunday Telegraph* because it had the best coverage. Brendan about hurling, in a way that sounded like polemic, even though he'd never held a stick in his life.

Mairead stood to go to the toilet, too fast, and knocked against Brendan's stool. Are you all right? Hugh said.

I'm bored to distraction.

You should have taken that lift, said Brendan.

She grabbed her bag and stalked towards the ladies. The barman was pushing a bottle bin along the corridor. She asked him for a cigarette and he offered her one from a packet with Polish writing on it.

How did you get yourself landed in this shithole? she said and went through the dim foyer to the front door. Evening had fallen low and thick over the village, and under the street lights the air glittered with damp. The cigarette burned her throat, and she tossed it on the footpath and started to walk.

She had put on suede pumps that were too wide for her, and her soles slapped off the road as she went down the hill towards her old house. The wind was piping through the straggly hedgerows and she could hardly see. She half-ran down the road and didn't slow until the security light came on. She let herself in. The newspaper and gun oil were still on the table. Hugh had left the radio on and a Romantic symphony was playing quietly from the speakers. She looked in the fridge. There was a bottle of wine, the stuff he bought her in the local shop that smelled like petrol. She poured a tumbler of it and went to the dresser to look at the photographs. In one he was a youth in a school blazer, looking affably mortified beside his parents. Another had been taken on the ramparts of a fort or castle, somewhere hot and dry and rocky. His hair was tied in a ponytail that looked wrong with his polo shirt and short chinos. In another he was sitting on a flowery chintz settee with a brown-haired woman. Two small girls were lying across them, laughing, as if they'd just been tickled.

She sat in an armchair. He'd never mentioned children. He knew about her two, away in Australia picking grapes or whatever it was they were doing. She had presumed he was free, unencumbered. Who was the woman in the photograph? They looked happy. Why was he here?

She woke with the glass tilted sideways across her stomach and Arthur's whiskers scratching the back of her hand. Hugh was standing over her.

What are you doing here? he said. Brendan nearly came back for a nightcap. What the hell were you thinking?

I was thinking I'd rather be fucking anywhere than in that house with him.

She got out of the chair. He stepped back and was looking at her top. There was a dark stain on it where she'd slopped wine over herself.

This isn't a good idea. He's going to find out, said Hugh. There were too many close calls today.

I couldn't give two shites.

Well, you should. He'll be home now, wondering where you are.

He'll not even notice.

It isn't right. He's a good guy, and I feel like an utter bastard.

He has you well fooled if you think he's one of the good guys. She went to the dresser and picked up the photo of the woman and children. She stabbed her finger into the woman's face. Who's she, when she's at home?

She's my wife.

You have a bloody wife! Did you not think to tell me?

We were having problems. I came here for a break.

Fuck's sake. What problems were they?

I was seeing someone else.

Jesus. Is this what you do?

That's a little sanctimonious, don't you think? Mairead slammed the photo face down on the shelf. Steady on, he said.

She picked up her bag and stumbled across the room to the back door. I've only been with two men, she said, and you're one of them.

She left the door open, thinking he'd come after her, beg her to stay. She was barely on the tarmac when she heard it click shut. Out on the road, she bent into the wind and rain, clutching her bag to her chest, sometimes walking, sometimes running, until she reached the main street.

The hotel was still open. She went into the lounge. The barman was putting chairs upside down on the tables. He went behind the bar and put his hands flat on the counter.

Are you trying to go home? she said.

It's OK for twenty minutes.

She ordered a brandy and sat by the fire. Her clothes were soaking, the wet fabric giving up the scent of scorched heather, Hugh's smell. Brendan had brought her up the glen not long after they'd met. He'd told her the story about the last day of the grouse, and they had stood on the moor and listened to the wind in the scrub. He led her to the spot where he'd buried the body and said she was the only one in the world he'd ever told. It was years before she understood he had told her the secret to bind her to him, to this place. The search team were preparing to move to the western slope. She hadn't just told them the general area. She had stood in the shadow of the high hanging rock of the tor and paced out her steps, three whins across to the base of the youngest holly tree, before calling the confidential number from her mobile. They would find the remains in the next day or so.

She went outside and stood on the street. Lights dotted the lower fields on the outskirts of the village. She couldn't see the glen, just the black loom of it, the dark mass of rock and bog and secrets. She stepped on to the road as a car with a jazzed-up northern plate sped past, and the passenger rolled down his window and shouted something at her. She crossed the street after it, rainwater fizzing up around her ankles, and started walking.

GARLAND SUNDAY

Orla's fingers worked through the leaves, picking off the fruit one by one, dropping them into the plastic bag that hung from her wrist. *Fraochán*, whinberry, myrtle, bilberry. She put one in her mouth and bit down. It was juicy and tart. When she had enough for a cake, she took out secateurs and began to cut. Soon she had filled a garden refuse sack with branches. She made her way across to the lip of the ridge. The hillside sliced down towards the road, shorn like a lawn by the sheep that clung to it. In front of her, over fields and bog and a silver lake, were the hills of three counties. Behind her, the wind was blowing through the caves. She started along the path. It hadn't rained for days, and scree scattered under her feet, making her break into a run. She was panting when she reached her car. She put the bag into the boot and set off for home.

On the bend beyond the hill, Orla had to pull up on a grass bank to let a truck pass. She was outside the Lavin place, a cottage with a tin roof and a glossy red door that her father-in-law owned. Dog roses brushed the whitewashed walls. A hydrangea hedge separated it from a triangle of ground furred with bright moss, a *cillín*. She had read somewhere that three corners were easier to defend against the fairies than four. There were no crosses or markings on the graves, just humps here and there, scarcely bigger than molehills. An unblessed place, for those buried with sin on them.

The driver of the truck beeped at her to edge forward on to the road. He was thickset, with a rose-gold cross around his neck. FOR ALL TENTS AND PURPOSES was printed on the side. He gave her a slow wink as he passed and she wondered was he the man who had come up with the slogan.

Orla took the bag of branches from the car and laid it on the patio table. She went into the kitchen through the back door and put the berries by the sink. The vacuum cleaner was going in one of the bedrooms; Kathy, the cleaner, didn't like to work around Jerry, who was at the table, his laptop open. There was a box of trophies and medals in front of him. Orla picked up a statuette, a brassy Atlas. *Sheaf Tossing, 1st Place* was engraved on the mahogany plinth beneath his feet.

The marquee people are there now, she said.

Right, said Jerry.

How's the speech going?

Getting there. He spread his shoulders so she couldn't see what he was typing.

Orla rinsed the bilberries in a colander. There were more than enough for a cake, so she put some in a pot with sugar and a piece of orange rind. The scent drew Kathy down the stairs. She stood by Orla at the stove and began to squash the fruit with the tip of a wooden spoon.

It's meant to have bits in it, said Orla.

Kathy let the spoon fall against the side of the pot and folded her arms. She was thirty-eight, a grandmother, and as petulant as an adolescent. She had been reared by her mother and brought up her own children alone. She viewed men with a suspicion Jerry found infuriating. Kathy never addressed him, never spoke to him at all. When he asked her to do something she cleared it with Orla first. Orla had told him it was reasonable to answer to one boss, but he said Kathy had the run of the place. As if to prove him right she filled the kettle and turned to Orla.

Cuppa, Mrs? she said.

Tea please, hun, said Orla. Jerry looked up sharply.

Orla pretended not to notice and stood tilting the pan from side to side on the hob until the tea was ready. Kathy banged a mug of instant coffee on to a coaster and pushed it at Jerry. She took a cigarette from her handbag and went out the back. Orla followed her with the tea.

She began to lay the branches across the patio table.

What are they for? said Kathy.

I'm going to twist them into a garland.

For what?

It's traditional.

My shite.

She was passing Orla the cigarette as Jerry opened the back door. Are you actually smoking? he said.

Shit, said Orla and handed it back. Jerry looked at them for a few seconds and went inside.

Kathy winced on the last drag and flicked the butt into the gutter. I'd have told him to blow it up his own arse, she said.

They heard doors slam at the front of the house, the engine of the jeep.

Come on and we'll make a cake, said Orla.

She had found a recipe for bilberry cake on the Internet, posted by someone called Tansey from a Slow Food group in Wicklow. It was for a butter sponge spotted with fruit, *traditionally presented by a girl to the boy she likes on Garland Sunday*. Orla took down the big brown pudding bowl that had belonged to her mother. She had left some butter out of the fridge overnight and it flopped into the bowl. Kathy pressed her finger into it.

I love butter. We were reared on marg, she said.

So were we, said Orla. She took the dry ingredients from the larder and began to weigh them. Kathy sieved the sugar. They took turns to beat it into the butter. When the mixture was pale and light they added eggs, a little at a time. Orla showed Kathy how to cut and fold in the flour. On the last turn they added the berries. The batter was glossy, streaked with magenta juices. Orla scraped it into a heart-shaped tin and put it in the oven.

Kathy licked the bowl. It's not as bad as I thought it would be, she said. What's the story with the cake anyway?

I'm going to carry it to the caves tomorrow and present it to Jerry.

Good luck with that.

Is it that obvious?

He has some puss on him, said Kathy. How are the lads getting on?

Great, I presume. I've hardly heard from them, she said. Orla's sons were at a surfing camp in the Mayo Gaeltacht. Will you come up to the caves yourself?

I'll stay in the field with the kids. I don't like it up there.

It's beautiful. I went up this morning to pick the berries.

It's an awful place. There's a woman in the town who brought her child up there and killed it with a stone.

Are you serious?

I'd hardly make something like that up.

How come I never heard it before?

You're a blow-in.

But surely that would have made it to the national news?

Not in those days. They covered everything up.

Why did she do it?

Baby blues. I had them after Sienna. The shit that goes through your head.

And she's walking around the place?

She was in the mentaller for years. They let her out when she was harmless.

That's horrific, said Orla.

I feel sorry for her. It gets in on you, that. I thought I was going nuts.

Kathy waited for Orla to answer. After the twins, her hormones had crashed so badly she was still taking anti-depressants, fourteen years later. Kathy had surely seen the pills; they were on her nightstand. God love her, was all Orla said.

Kathy left to finish the bedrooms; Orla made butter-cream and washed up. It had been her idea to include old customs in the Garland Sunday celebrations this year. She thought it would please Jerry, but now she fretted that no one but her would make a cake or weave a garland, that things between them would get even worse. When the timer sounded, she took the cake out and put it on a wire rack to cool. She had planned to make it when Jerry was home, fill the house with the smell of baking, hold the wooden spoon to his lips and watch him taste it. But Jerry wasn't here; couldn't, in fact, stand to be in the same room as her. How would he be when she presented him with the cake? A heart-shaped cake, at that. It was over five months since the termination, as she called it, the other word horrifying to her. Jerry had booked the flights, travelled with her; he hadn't wanted another baby either. But something had begun to change in the months since. Rancour gathering in him that he wouldn't be drawn on.

After Kathy left, Orla took four containers of food from the fridge. She brought them out to the car and drove the mile and a half to her father-in-law's house, up a drive of close-cut leylandii. The house was a split-level bungalow wrapped in a veranda that looked up towards the caves. He was waiting when she got out of the car. There's nothing wrong with your hearing, said Orla. She kissed his cheek. It was smooth and cool.

I was putting out the ashes, he said. I heard the engine.

She followed him around the side of the house. The brass coal scuttle was by the back door, full. She resisted the urge to carry it indoors. She had been trying to persuade him to install a gas stove, but he insisted on burning smoky coal and turf in an open grate. He said it was company.

I have a few dinners for your freezer, said Orla.

Meals on Wheels for the geriatric.

Some geriatric, she said. Today he was wearing a pale blue shirt with a soft collar, a dark red lambswool V-neck over it. He shopped in the last department store in town, an Edwardian building where he bought Donegal tweed jackets for winter and linen trousers for summer. Orla had told Jerry she would only marry him if he could guarantee he would age like his father. He hadn't. His looks came from his mother, who had died at sixty-three, sagging with disappointment.

How are the lads getting on?

Great. We're allowed phone them in the morning.

They weren't sent home for speaking English, anyway.

No. I nearly wish they had been. It's so quiet without them.

He opened the fridge and took out a bottle of white wine.

I shouldn't, she said.

The glass he gave her had a silver chain around the stem with a pink crystal charm attached. The house was full of such flummery; Brenda McCarrick had been a woman of girly tastes that were incongruous now with Michael's lone male presence. As the rooms needed to be decorated, Orla steered him towards sober colours, but there was still enough of Brenda around the place to make it look fluffy.

Michael poured himself a whiskey. He held it up at her.

Cheers, said Orla. The wine was yellow and oily, and the glass rang like a tiny bell when she tilted it to her mouth.

He took a cigar from the drawer in the dresser and offered her a Benson & Hedges from a pack he kept for visitors. Orla didn't think anyone but her ever smoked one. They went through the sitting room and out to the veranda. They sat on a wooden bench and he lit her cigarette. What am I like? she said.

You'll quit when you're ready. Is Jerry at the field?

Yes. We're trying new stuff this year, she said. Well, old stuff. I picked bilberries on the hill and baked them into a cake. And cut branches for a garland. Orla had never enjoyed the festival, a celebration so embedded in the townland that just walking around the field made her feel as though she was trespassing. It was a measure of the peril she believed her marriage to be in that she was throwing herself into the preparations.

It's years since I saw anyone bring a cake up there, he said.

Kathy helped me bake it. She told me a mad story about a woman who killed her baby up at the caves.

Did she?

You know Kathy. Did anyone ever present a cake to you?

A cloud had moved in front of the sun and the hedgerows below the caves darkened to a deep petrol blue.

Michael toked on his cigar, opening and closing his mouth like a fish. He didn't answer.

Jerry had been and gone. The trophies had been tidied into a box. The speech was open on his laptop. It began with thanks, acknowledging the committee, the sponsors, the judges. She saw her own name, then. *Lastly, big thanks to my wife Orla for judging the Bonny Baby Contest.* She went outside to the table and set about making the garland. She spread the branches out and chose the fullest, the freshest. She stripped the lower leaves and began to wind them together, keeping the rough edges to the back, taking more switches, twisting and bending, using florist's wire to fix them. When she was finished, her hands were stinging and sticky with blood. Jerry was going to surround her with babies. She hadn't realised until now how angry he was.

He came home after seven. She found a packet of prawns in the freezer and within minutes put a passable pasta dish on the table. He said he had eaten already and went to the sitting room with a bottle of beer. She ate a couple of forkfuls from the pot. She went to bed and read for a while. It was a book about a sick woman whose estranged mother came to sit for a few days by her hospital bed. The woman talked about her marriage failing, how much she had hurt her children. Orla closed the book. It was too sad. She was still awake when Jerry came in. He undressed and lay with his back to her. She reached her hand towards him but hesitated, wondering where on his body she could lay it. She drew it back.

She was icing the cake in her dressing gown when he got up.

The boys are expecting us to phone early, she said. She dialled and handed him her mobile.

Well, buck, he said. Are you fluent yet? He went outside. From the window, she watched him roll a torn sliotar back and forward under the ball of his foot, his face sometimes tender, sometimes amused. He came back into the kitchen.

Here's your mother, now. Be good, he told the phone.

She found the boys taciturn, and hoped it was because they had already told their father all their news. Jonny had always been Jerry's, earnest and stolid like him. Luke had been hers, restless and fearful, traits that beguiled her as much as they worried his father. But Jerry had worked at him, with hours building pirate ships from Lego, endless pitching of ball to stick. The bond they now had confounded her. She hadn't seen it coming.

Love you, she told each of them. She put the phone down and pinched the web between her thumb and forefinger. She let go when she no longer felt like crying.

Jerry ate a bowl of cereal standing up at the sink, supping milk and staring at the garden. He left before ten. Orla went upstairs and lay down again. She had slept badly, on her left side, the wrong side, rather than look at Jerry's back. She picked up the book she was reading. The woman said something was 'not right' in her marriage, that she waited until her girls were grown and then left her husband. Orla tossed the book across the bed. Things were not right in lots of marriages, but not everyone could shag a jazz musician and move into an apartment in Brooklyn. She drew herself into the shape she usually slept in, on her right side, knees pulled up towards her belly. Her left hand around her right breast, where Jerry's hand should have been.

The previous year the weather had been so bad they had to cram everything into the marquee, but the day was bright and gusty. Halfway up the hill that overlooked the field, the caves sat like a row of blackened teeth, the outline of the cairn just visible high above them. She went into the tent. Jerry was at the far end, standing just in front of the stage with Father Horan. Orla waved at him. He lifted his chin in reply. Along one side, trestle tables had been covered with white cloth. She carried her cake and garland over and laid them out. For a few minutes they were conspicuous, all alone on the table, but soon three elderly women arrived laden with cakes on pretty china stands, woven foliage thrown around their necks like feather boas.

Orla went to the refreshment table to get them each a cup of tea. A man in his twenties with slicked-back hair and a black Western-style shirt was on the stage. He stepped up to the microphone and began to count. One two, one two. His voice was deeper than his slight build suggested, his accent American. Beside Orla, a girl with heavy make-up was setting out a display of CDs. The singer was on the cover. *Ethan Magee. The Singin' Brickie.*

Are you in charge of the fan club? Orla asked her.

I'm Ethan's fiancée, the girl said, twisting at her ring finger. There was no ring on it.

He sang the chorus of 'Help Me Make It Through the Night' and came down off the stage. The girl put her arms around his neck and kissed him as if he was returning from war. The Singin' Brickie peeled her away and frowned at the bronzer she had left on his black satin shirt. He nodded at the display.

Shift the whole cunting lot of them, he said. His accent Fermanagh now, or maybe Cavan.

Orla sidled through the crowd with her tray. The rest of the local Irish Countrywomen's Association branch had brought cakes and garlands. They had Jerry surrounded.

Blessed art thou amongst women, said Orla. He smiled grimly.

Someone had put boxes of different sizes under the cloth. The cakes were at different heights now, like a wedding breakfast in a fairy tale. One was iced in white and scattered with garnet-coloured rose petals. Another was a dark chocolate sponge filled with cream and berries, like a Black Forest gateau. Someone else had made a pavlova. Jerry came and stood beside her. It looks well, Orla, he said. He was only speaking to her because they had an audience.

He went to the stage and took the microphone. At first, he had to compete with the tuneless *nyaaas* that were being wrenched from the whistles and fiddles and boxes of the Comhaltas children. The crowd settled as he went through the health and safety announcements, and the joke he cracked at Father Horan's expense got a few laughs and made the minuscule cleric smirk pinkly. She hardly knew him at all.

Out in the field, the games and contests had begun. Orla took photographs that she would send to the boys later, of children dancing with brushes, singing ballads, playing reels on ornate concertinas. The tug of war was generating even more crude puns than the sheaf tossing. Kathy's daughter Cody was watching it, in a group of older teenagers. Kathy must have been looking after the baby again. Around the field, the haycocks and pikes were gathered up, boards lifted. People were moving towards the tent for the last event before the race, the Bonny Baby Contest. She followed them.

Jerry was waiting by the stage. Orla took her place between the other judges: the public health nurse and an independent councillor called Linda with permed blonde hair who had been elected on a manifesto of 'Fitness!' and Tidy Towns. They each had a page printed with a table of criteria: smiliness, grooming, temperament, cuteness and bonniness. Eleven babies wriggled in their mothers' arms, except for baby number seven, Kayleigh Rose Mannion, who was sleeping on the shoulder of her grandmother, Kathy. Contestants had to be aged from six to eighteen months; the previous year they had disqualified a strapping girl of at least two who Jerry said could have won the sheaf-throwing contest.

One after the other, Jerry led the women up the steps. The mothers and babies had been told to wear black T-shirts and paused in front of a screen to be photographed. When the boys were tiny, Orla had professional pictures taken by a young Italian photographer in Dublin. The girl persuaded her to take her top off and swaddle them in a sheet, holding them to her as if she was nursing them. Orla had gone along with it but hated the photographs as soon as she saw them: her expressionless look, the shadows on her face. She hadn't managed to breastfeed the boys. A midwife had declared her nipples 'inverted and unsuitable'. The words were said casually, before Orla knew that what was wrong with her was depression and not a general unsuitability for motherhood.

Kathy carried Kayleigh up the steps. She minced across the stage and posed for a photo in her pink fleece. A cheer went up.

She's some article, said a man's voice behind her. Orla twisted around to look at him. It was Michael. There was such kindness in his eyes she knew at once. Jerry had told him about the abortion.

They had flown to Liverpool from Knock, at every turn waiting to hear a voice from home. They hired a car at John Lennon Airport and drove to Stockport, checking into a Premier Inn beside an industrial estate. Men in their shirtsleeves with biros in their breast pockets were sitting around the bar. Orla and Jerry nursed gins they couldn't drink and went out for Indian food they couldn't eat. In the morning Jerry walked her into the clinic by the hand. There was a protestor outside, a distracted man with a Cork accent. He was holding a child's doll, a nude peachy thing slathered in red nail polish that looked like its face had been melted. He thrust it at Orla as she passed, pulled at her coat, begged her not to go in.

When Jerry left, she sat in the waiting room and tidied her handbag. Folded receipts. Packed stray tissues back into their plastic sleeve. She fixated on ordinary things. The watercolour of a vase of tulips hanging above the information stand. The bangle of tiny stars tattooed

around the receptionist's wrist. The doctor's Nature
Treks. How very white they were, the faint squelch of
the left heel. But there were things she couldn't keep
out. The sobs from the teenage girl on the trolley next
to her in the recovery room when she came round and
asked to see her baby. The glint of the tiny silver feet
Orla and her friends had worn on their school blazers.
The sense that she wasn't the person she had thought
she was.

For a couple of weeks afterwards she had lain about
the house, sleeping and dreaming. Jerry fussed over her,
worried she was sick, that something had gone wrong.
He filled hot-water bottles and took her temperature.
The procedure had left her feeling weak, she told him,
that was all. It wasn't true. She was squeamish. Horrified.

The babies had begun to complain, soothers, breasts and
bottles being pushed into their mouths.

By the way, what is 'bonniness'? said Orla.

It's kind of like cuteness, said Linda.

Cuteness is down here already, said Orla.

I'd say it's the X factor. Something you can't put your
finger on, said the nurse.

That'll do, said Orla.

They totted up the scores. Kayleigh and a baby boy
with hair like Leonardo DiCaprio as Gatsby were tied
for first place.

Kayleigh's mother isn't wearing a black T-shirt, said Linda.

She's the grandmother, said Orla and the nurse in unison.

Where's the mother? said Linda.

Ah here, said the nurse. I'm voting for Kayleigh.

So am I, said Orla.

Linda went to Jerry with the result. He frowned and followed Linda up the steps.

It was a very difficult decision, as all the babies are beautiful, but today we have a winner. Kayleigh Rose Mannion! said Linda. She whooped and punched the air.

That one. You'd swear she'd voted for her, said the nurse.

Kathy accepted flowers and a voucher. She and her granddaughter held themselves regally as Jerry led them off the stage.

The cakes and garlands were gathered from the tables and those who were able began the steep trek up the hillside. Michael fell into step beside Orla, stopping sometimes to catch his breath. A group of women and children passed, smiling, carrying their handmade offerings. Fair play to you, Orla, he said. She wondered what he must think of her and couldn't look at him.

They heard the crack of a starting gun. The runners began streaming from the field on to the path that led up the other side of the mountain, each of them carrying a stone to replace any that may have been taken away. Sometimes the sky blue of Jerry's vest flashed into view.

The historian led them into the largest cave. They closed around him where he stood silhouetted against the landscape, just inside the jagged mouth. He admired the garlands and cakes, and told of the early Christians, how they had clung to their pagan customs and feasts, melding them into the festivals we still celebrate. Christmas. Easter. Hallowe'en. Garland Sunday. That this was a sacred place there was no doubt, he said. It was in the bones they had found. A bear skull, deer and hare and wolf bones. Seal bones and oyster shells carried thirty miles from the coast. A pile of horse teeth. He told stories. Of the infant Cormac Mac Airt, born by a well at the foot of the hill, stolen by a she-wolf and reared with her cubs. Of Fionn and the Fianna, hunting for Diarmuid and Gráinne in the caves, only to be spindled awry with holly by three hags of the Tuath Dé Danaan until they lay impotent on the cold limestone. Orla thought of Kathy's lurid tale of infanticide, the mad mother who had to be locked away. Stories of unearthly women, lurking in the dark amongst bones and ashes. What of Orla, the child she'd refused to bear? How had Jerry told the story to his father? Who else had he told?

The runners came into the cave, then, on their way back down the hill. The clock was stopped while they

drank water. Those with cakes were asked to step forward
and find the object of their affection. Orla began edging
to the front. Jerry was near the back, making it hard for
her. Cakes were handed over amidst blushes and giggles.
Orla was the last woman in the circle. Step out where
we can see you, Jerry, said the historian. You're amongst
friends. Someone laughed.

Orla had dreaded the moment for days, that Jerry
would turn the cold look on her in front of everyone,
that they would sense he was punishing her and wonder
what she'd done. She held the cake out, daring him to
refuse it. She didn't care any more. He took it from
her and kissed her cheek. She walked away. When the
runners were setting off again, he tried to give it back
to her.

Will you carry it to the car? he said.

Nope, she said. It's all yours.

Orla and Michael descended the mountain without
speaking. They went straight to the bar. How did Jerry
get on jogging with the cake, do you think? he said,
handing her a plastic cup of wine.

He probably fecked it into the brambles as soon as I
was out of sight.

Kathy came to join them.

Congrats, Granny, said Orla. Kayleigh was a few feet
away, drooling her new-found celebrity over her mother's shoulder.

Thanks. How did you get on with the cake? said Kathy.

Fabulous. I was the last to present one, and everyone looking at us.

Sap.

I know. And I couldn't stop thinking about that awful story you told me. Poor woman must have been demented.

We're all demented, said Kathy.

Orla accepted the cigarette Kathy offered. I'll buy you a packet, she said.

Proper order. She flounced away towards the tent as if she knew they were looking at her.

Orla smoked until her throat was hot. She ground the butt under her foot and followed Michael into the marquee. Jerry was by the stage in his running gear. He raised an arm at them in salute.

The Singin' Brickie was in full voice, holding the final note of 'Delilah' for an implausibly long time, cutting it off to whoops and whistles. He wiped his face with a flannel and threw it at the crowd. One of the ICA women caught it. He pointed at her and swung the cable of his microphone in the air like a lasso.

Jerry joined them. Will you have another drink? he said. His voice was loud, but the look on his face betrayed him. Tight, as if he was trying to find a way in.

Are you having one? she asked Michael.

I might head on, he said. I'm feeling my age.

I'll jump in with you, said Orla.

Michael said goodnight to Jerry and excused himself through the crowd. Jerry hovered in front of Orla.

We need to talk, he said.

Jesus, she said. She turned to leave and he put his hand on her arm. The left hand with the wedding ring on it and the gingery down above the knuckles. You're ready to unburden yourself, is that it? You can fuck off.

She went outside and got into Michael's car. He had bought himself a Saab as a retirement present. It was twelve years old now; the leather seats still smelled new.

There were children playing in the field, careening into each other in various stages of sugar rush. She hadn't been here without the twins before. She felt their absence. The ache of time already passed.

Jerry told me, you know, said Michael. About that business in Liverpool.

I thought as much. I suppose you think I'm a monster.

I think it must have been very hard for you.

He turned out on to the road. On the bend for home, he pulled in by the Lavin place.

Why are we stopping here?

A girl lived in this house. Mary-Kate Lavin. Baby, they called her, because she was the youngest. One year she made me a cake, said Michael.

I thought you were being cagey when I asked you, all right.

Have you time for a nightcap? he said. I want to tell you a story.

When they got to the house, Michael poured them each a drink, Orla asking for gin, to avoid the wine he'd opened yesterday. He got coats for them both and they went on to the veranda. The sun was low over the west side of the mountain, washing the limestone in pink light.

I'm listening, she said.

When he had finished speaking it was almost dark, the sky streaked purple and orange. Inside, Michael went along the hall to his office and came back with a box file. There was a large notebook with a blue-black cover like mussel shells and a couple of photographs. A bundle of paper, foolscap size rather than A4. The typewriter keys had been struck hard and the words were in slight relief, like Braille. There were pages and pages.

She sent Jerry a message, asking him to pick her up on his way home. He came to the house just after eleven. Michael was quiet when he arrived.

You're worn out from going up the hill, Jerry said, but he hadn't heard the story. He hadn't seen what it had taken for him to tell it.

Kathy was delighted with her win, he said when they got home.

You're all chat now, is that it? I'm going to bed, she said.

I thought we could talk.

OK then. Let's talk about the contest, and why you put me down as a judge.

I thought you might like it.

You're full of shit. You wanted to punish me.

This has been hard for me as well.

Don't I know it.

Upstairs, she took off her make-up and smeared night cream across her face, over her loose jawline and the rucks between her eyes. She was forty-nine. When she was having the twins it had said 'elderly primigravida' on her chart at the hospital. She could think of nothing worse than being pregnant. Or mothering another child.

Jerry came into the room after one. She pretended to be asleep but watched him change out of his clothes in the moonlight. He took his trousers off, his shirt, his underwear, movements slower when he had to bend over the ball of fat at his middle. She closed her eyes while he put his pyjamas on; it was hard to take a man seriously in only his socks. He got in beside her and put his hand on her shoulder, tilting her back so he could look at her.

I'm sorry, he said.

I'm not, said Orla. I'm not sorry at all. She rolled back on to her side and pulled the duvet tightly around herself. For the first time in months she slept all night.

She woke at seven and went downstairs. She sat at the kitchen table with the pile of papers. When she had read them all she made tea and began again. The first document was a medical report. They noted the woman's state. Agitated, at times almost elated. She had spoken for several hours without stopping. Baby Lavin's demise had begun on Garland Sunday, when she climbed the hill in her blue dress with the lace collar and presented the cake to Michael McCarrick. Or maybe it began before that, when she baked it, with so much hope in her heart. After Michael had laughed, refusing to take the cake from her, she went back down the hill to the field. She wanted to run home to her father but made herself stay and not show her shame. Something happened with the boys afterwards, she said. She found them looking at her, sideways looks. Banter started, little jokes. One of them offered her some whiskey. She put it to her mouth and drank. She liked how it made her feel, how the burn of it faded to a heat that ran through her limbs, loosened her lips. She heard herself talk and she didn't sound like herself. She was funny, she said. The boys lingered nearer, especially an older lad called Noel Scanlon.

Michael left not long after the sun went down. She felt his eyes on her but didn't look back. Served him right for shaming her. The other boys liked her, so she didn't care. The whiskey bottle was in her hand again and she drank long this time. *Leave her. Don't give her any more*, someone said. She felt dizzy and stumbled over to the wall. She rested against it and closed her eyes, waited until the feeling stopped. But it didn't stop. She went across the gravel to the edge of the field and pulled her knickers down. She missed and felt a hot trickle on her thigh. She had nothing to wipe herself with and rocked back and forth until she was dry. She heard a small cough and stood up. It was Noel Scanlan. He put out a hand to steady her. Her pants were still around her knees, and she staggered away from him to pull them up. He laughed and turned his back while she arranged herself. She sat on the wall again. They were alone. She wanted to go home, she told him. She was shivering. He passed her the bottle, the rest of the whiskey. *There's only a drop*, he said. *It'll warm you*. She didn't remember anything after that.

At cockcrow she woke in the cow byre behind the cottage. She went into the house quietly. She tried to take her dress off, but it was buttoned wrongly. Then her slip. Her breasts were tender, as though the nipples had been pinched. The skin on her thighs was tight with dried blood and milky stuff. She was sore. Inside her was sore. She stayed in bed until she heard her father moving about downstairs. He hadn't noticed she was late. He asked her about the cake. She told him Michael was delighted with it then fled to the garden.

Scanlan came to the gate in the afternoon. He was talking low, leaning into her ear. When he looked at her his face was dog-hungry. He terrified her. *We were half mad*, he said. *Do you mind it, the way we were?* She couldn't remember anything. Maybe she was half mad. He kept coming back, every day for weeks. He asked her about her time of the month, knew more about her bloods than she did. He wouldn't see her stuck, he said. He went to speak to her father. He promised he wouldn't tell her father she was expecting, but she knew he had. Her father wouldn't look at her after. He never looked her in the eyes again.

There was innocence in the voice that was left on the page, a child's way of processing the horror of her circumstances, of the degradation of life with Noel Scanlan. She didn't know what he had done to her until he did it to her again, on the wedding night. *At me*, she said. *He was at me all the time.* The baby had arrived late, too big to come out by himself. They left her writhing on a rubber sheet for two days before they pulled him out of her. She had called for her mother, so beside herself she had forgotten her mother was dead. Scanlan was at her again the night they let her home.

Scanlan called the baby Pascal because he came on Good Friday. When the midwife showed him to her his face was closed and red. She tried to love him. She went to the ward and stared at him for hours. She watched his face open over the week, until one day he turned and Scanlan was looking back at her. She had shrieked. *He looked at me*, she told the midwife. The woman had laughed. *He couldn't look at you if he wanted to*, she said. *He can't see.* But Baby knew what she saw. After that she closed her eyes when she fed him. He was greedy, guzzling at her until she was raw. At night, his father would take over, ramming into her. The baby grew and grew. His head, that had hurt her on the way out, appalled her, and his white, meaty limbs. She fed them and cleaned up after them, but there wasn't enough of her to go around. When the child cried the sound went through her and there was a pain behind her eyes that never went away. She stopped sleeping and everything was louder, brighter.

She went to her father. To tell him about the baby, how he was suckling the very life out of her. About Scanlan, pestering her around the house. He stayed quiet while she spoke. There was a rim of grime on the collar of his shirt. He was never like that when she looked after him. She told him she would come back to do his washing. You've yourself well enough landed where you are, he said. Take yourself back into town and get on with it.

She went home. The baby cried and cried. She mashed spuds for him with butter and he ate so much he was sick. She gave him her own dinner. Scanlan was agitated, telling her to keep the child quiet, that she must be doing something wrong if she couldn't shut him up. She gave the baby Carnation milk in a sauce bottle with a teat on it. He drank it all, but still he cried. She put her breast into his mouth. His teeth had come on early and she felt a slice of pain and pulled him away. He drew blood, she told the police later, but the only blood they found was on the baby's towel, a bright red squirt that had bubbled from his lungs.

Jeremiah McCarrick, Michael's father, had sat with Baby Lavin through the police questioning. Interviewed her, although, as the medical report stated, no one had to ask any questions. She talked and talked. He recorded what she told him longhand in the notebook. And then he handed it over to Michael, to read each word and type the story. Jeremiah knew he had refused the cake.

Orla tidied away the papers. Poor Michael. His anguish was on the pages, in the print, bold at times, more often slight, where he could hardly bear to strike the keys. He was nineteen, Baby Lavin a year younger. When they asked her if she knew what she had done, she answered yes. She knew well what she had done. The child wasn't right, she said. He wasn't right. She thanked them very much for listening.

Orla went out to Jerry's car. Her garland was across the back seat, wilted, the cake beside it. He had carried it down the mountain after all. She brought them into the kitchen. Michael had bought the Lavin place when Baby's father died. The land was leased to a sheep farmer, but

Michael paid someone to cut the grass and look after the house. He thought that if Baby was ever released from hospital she would want to live there. Scanlan had left town and become a prison officer, and the house where the baby died had become a hairdressing studio. Baby was released to sheltered accommodation after thirty years. Michael had gone to see her once. She was outside her little bungalow, smoking. The ivory complexion was dull, and there was a tar-stained quiff at her widow's peak. She was vague and fat. He told her he would come back and she shook her head. She died from lung cancer three years later.

Orla took the photographs from the box. They were stiff and matt, from a time when being photographed was momentous. Formal compositions, the subjects looking directly at the camera. Baby as a little girl, her mother and older brothers around her. Baby in a floral dress with a wide skirt, as Michael must have remembered her, holding her father's arm. Orla spread out the garland. She wrought it around the kitchen dresser to frame the shelves. She placed a photograph in the centre where the foliage was fullest, freshest, twisting branches around it to secure it. It was of Baby Lavin holding Pascal Scanlan. The look on her face was of affront, surprise. Spun awry, she and her poor doomed infant.

She hadn't killed him with a stone at the caves. She left her father's house and pushed the big pram all the way back to town. After the feeding and the vomiting and more feeding and the griping from Scanlan and the way he was looking at her she brought the child into the bathroom. She filled the bath with water and tested it with her elbow. She held his head back and washed his hair. She turned him over and washed his back. She was still holding him face down when Scanlan found them twenty minutes later.

Jerry came into the kitchen.

What are you up to? he said.

I'm reading.

He went to the dresser. Who's that?

It's a long story.

Come back to bed, will you? I'll bring us up tea.

She went upstairs and got under the covers. She opened her book. The woman had resigned herself to carrying sadness through her life. Like the rest of us, Orla thought, and what of it? It didn't mean we would do anything differently.

He came in carrying a tray that he put on his night-stand. There was a plate with two wedges of the cake she had baked for him.

So you ran down the hill with the cake in your hand.

I walked. I came last in the race.

A piece of purple-stained sponge fell away as he handed her a slice. Kathy only changed those sheets the other day, she said.

She was aware of the crumbs in the bed as he told her again he was sorry. She could feel them under her arse when he spread her legs with his knee. They were under her thighs, the faintest scuffing, as he worked himself in.

Does this mean we're all right? he said.

It means we're having sex, she said. Brisk, wordless sex. As if there were children in the house.

ACKNOWLEDGEMENTS

So many people helped me write this book. Thank you.

To the Arts Council of Northern Ireland for financial assistance and Damian Smyth for unwavering support and encouragement.

To the Sandy Field Writers for not laughing at my excruciating early attempts, especially Norah McGillen, Rhona Trench, Julianna Holland and Máiread McCann; Niamh MacCabe for dragging me along when I didn't know I wanted to write.

To the humans of the Seamus Heaney Centre at Queens University Belfast, in particular Garrett Carr, who oversaw the writing of this collection with patience, generosity and humour, and has helped me way beyond the call of duty.

To the editors who published some of these stories: Declan Meade and Sally Rooney of *The Stinging Fly*, John Lavin of *The Lonely Crowd*, Eimear Ryan, Laura Jane Cassidy and Claire Hennessey of *Banshee*, Olivia Smith and Kevin Barry of *Winter Papers*. Extra special thanks to Michael Nolan of *The Tangerine* for his acuity, decency and big-heartedness, and for pretending I'm cool enough to call him my friend.

To the brilliant Sarah-Jane Forder, who had the unenviable task of copy-editing this collection. You were delightful to work with and it's a far better book for your sharp eye and gentle manner.

To everyone at Bloomsbury, especially Ros Ellis, Lauren Whybrow, Jasmine Horsey, Cormac Kinsella; Greg Heinimann for the unreal cover.

To my amazing editor, Alexis Kirschbaum, for taking a punt on this ould one and changing her life. I still can't believe it.

To my kind, intelligent and rather marvellous agent, Eleanor Birne – how lucky am I? – and all at PEW Literary.

To Celine Connell, Pat Webb, Rose Jordan, Philippa Neave, Bernardine Hanratty, Peter O'Connell.

To Una Mannion for taking my daily histrionic phone calls and for being the best kind of first reader; for your example, integrity and plain goodness, and for telling me I could when I thought I couldn't.

To Fleur and Alan for putting me up and putting up with me.

To John and Lorna. Carlsberg don't do in-laws, but if they did...

To my family, for all the love and divilment: Joanne, Dave, Sinead, Paul, Johnny, John, Brenda; the nephew and the nieces.

To my children, Tom and Anna, for being the best possible distraction.

To Stephen, for everything.

A NOTE ON THE AUTHOR

LOUISE KENNEDY grew up in Holywood, Co. Down. Her short stories have been published in *The Stinging Fly*, *The Tangerine*, *The Lonely Crowd and Banshee*. Her work has won the Ambit Short Fiction (2015), Wasifiri New Writing (2015), John O'Connor (2016) and Listowel Los-Gatos (2016) prizes. She is a PhD candidate at the Seamus Heaney Centre, Queens University Belfast. Before starting her writing career, she spent over twenty years working as a chef. She lives in Sligo with her husband and two children.

A NOTE ON THE TYPE

The text of this book is set in Perpetua. This typeface is an adaptation of a style of letter that had been popularised for monumental work in stone by Eric Gill. Large scale drawings by Gill were given to Charles Malin, a Parisian punch-cutter, and his hand-cut punches were the basis for the font issued by Monotype. First used in a private translation called 'The Passion of Perpetua and Felicity', the italic was originally called Felicity.